Blaze™

Dear Reader,

As a Blaze writer, I think about sexual situations a lot. It's part of my job, and let's face it, that's pretty fun! But when it came time to write Jessica's story, I discovered a character who didn't always have fun thinking about sexual situations. Because of a difficult past, sex had become problematic for her.

But because I'm a Blaze writer, I needed to help her out of that dark corner, and that's where Rocco Easton comes in. I loved writing about this hero whose career was stolen out from underneath him yet he still found a way to channel his talents into productive work. Rocco has faced plenty of dark corners himself.

I hope you'll enjoy Jessica's journey to new healing and her path to reclaiming her sensuality.

Happy reading!

Joanne Rock

UP CLOSE AND PERSONAL

Joanne Rock

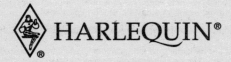

HARLEQUIN®

TORONTO • NEW YORK • LONDON
AMSTERDAM • PARIS • SYDNEY • HAMBURG
STOCKHOLM • ATHENS • TOKYO • MILAN • MADRID
PRAGUE • WARSAW • BUDAPEST • AUCKLAND

ISBN-13: 978-0-373-79399-0
ISBN-10:   0-373-79399-5

UP CLOSE AND PERSONAL

Copyright © 2008 by Joanne Rock.

www.eHarlequin.com

Printed in U.S.A.

ABOUT THE AUTHOR

After testing out careers in public relations, teaching, acting and journalism, Joanne Rock became a fiction writer to maintain sanity while sitting at home with three small children. Writing books quickly went from a temporary mental exercise to an addictive passion. After more than thirty books she hopes her sanity has been duly maintained. Joanne is a three-time RITA® Award winner, and her stories have been reprinted in twenty-four countries and translated into nineteen languages. She pens medieval historicals and sexy contemporaries from her home in the gorgeous Adirondack region of upstate New York, where she lives with her husband and sons. Learn more about Joanne and her work by visiting her at http://joannerock.com or at http://myspace.com/joanne_rock.

Books by Joanne Rock

HARLEQUIN BLAZE

HARLEQUIN HISTORICAL

*Single in South Beach
**West Side of Confidential
†The Wrong Bed
††Perfect Timing
‡Night Eyes

To Renee Halverson, whose dedication to writing has always been an inspiration. Thank you for being such a wonderful friend!

_1_

JESSICA WINSLOW NEEDED to arouse a room full of women.

Right here. Right now.

She took deep breaths in her small suite at the Hotel del Coronado in San Diego, an accommodation with no view of the spectacular oceanfront outside. She'd booked this spot as a prep space for the retreat weekend she was leading—her biggest business coup yet. Eight women had bought into the extravagant "Better in Bed" workshop offered by Jess's fledgling company. Who knew there would be so much interest in reclaiming your sensuality among wealthy, successful women who—seemingly—had the world at their collective feet?

"Do you need anything else, Ms. Winslow?"

A sleekly tanned young caterer with a Spanish accent tucked a clipboard under her arm as she waited for Jess's instructions.

"Everyone has drinks next door?" She hoped this first session of the weekend would be made a smidge easier by plying her guests with alcohol.

Hell, her discussion of erotic massage might be easier if _she_ downed the alcohol. She'd wanted to kick off the retreat with a bang, but planning the workshop in theory hadn't fully prepared her for the intimidation factor of teaching erotic massage to a roomful of strangers she desperately needed to impress.

"They've all been served and there is a small bar set up for refills like we discussed." The woman tapped her fuchsia-pink manicured fingernail down the itemized list on her clipboard. "Would you like me to bring you a glass of chardonnay?"

Jessica winced. Was her tension that obvious? There was no reason for the attack of nerves, since she knew her material backward and forward. Well, no reason except that setting her business venture apart from her family's million-and-one get-rich-quick schemes depended on the good word of mouth generated by the attendees of this workshop.

After being raised well below the poverty line by parents who skirted the law, the truant officer and even Social Services, Jessica craved the stability of her own business. And the fact that she was targeting well-to-do women was no coincidence. She drank up the sweet scent of security inherent in their money, even as she made certain she had something of value to offer in return. Her business, Up Close and Personal, was no get-rich-quick scam but a labor of love that spiraled out of her need to pass on the benefits of self-help training she'd received since escaping her past, her birth family and, later, her foster family.

The wealthy women in the ocean-view suites across the hall could make or break Jessica's new career with whatever they chose to share about this weekend at their respective country clubs come Monday morning.

Jess shook her head, refusing to give in to second-guessing. She'd have every woman in there eager to go home and jump the man of her choice. But to do that, she needed a clear head.

"No wine for me, thank you. We should be set until it's time to bring in the appetizers an hour from now." She checked her antique watch, unable to delay the inevitable.

The timepiece slid around her wrist as she left the safety of her room; the jewelry a long-ago gift from her father. One of the few he'd purchased honestly, since he'd found it at a garage sale. Because of her rocky relationship with her lawless parents, she wore the piece to remind herself she would forge a future all her own. On her own.

Passing a young family dressed in their bathing suits in the hall, Jessica pasted on her public face. She opened the door to the retreat space, ready to teach her guests everything she knew about erotic massage and reclaiming your sensuality.

Jessica hadn't had a lot of opportunity to test her skills on real people, but she knew the methods worked, since she could at least talk about sex again and feel the hormone rush of getting turned-on.

Five years ago, she hadn't been able to do either. A date rape in her teens had haunted her long after the night she'd been sexually assaulted by her date.

"Welcome, ladies!"

The scent of the surf hit her along with the floral fragrances of a half-dozen bouquets she'd ordered scattered around the room for ambiance. The whole suite had also been draped in burgundy taffeta at her request. The dark colors and bright flowers were offset by the moody purple light of the sunset bleeding through the sheer curtains, but soon the walls would be lit solely by two cast-iron candelabra she'd brought here in the back of her Escalade.

The vehicle and the accessories were both part of her belief that image was everything in a business like this. High-end consumers didn't show up for retreat weekends at bargain hotels, and they didn't expect their speaker to roll up in a decade-old sedan. No matter that the payments on that damn Escalade were killing her bank account. The cost of the accessories and the hotel space meant she would only break even this weekend, but if it generated more business—

Where the hell were her students? Jessica was so busy admiring the way the decor came together that she hadn't immediately noticed her workshop clients were not in the room.

"Honey, will you look at the torso on that one?"

A woman's voice floated in from the balcony, followed by a chorus of feminine sighs. Curious—and needing to keep her evening activities on schedule—Jessica headed toward the terrace hidden by a wall of sheer curtains and French doors.

"I'd like to give an erotic massage to him," another voice chimed in.

Stepping out onto the balcony, Jessica could see eight women's backs as they jockeyed for a spot at the railing. Silk- and linen-clad hips jostled while manicured hands held a variety of brightly colored drinks aloft to keep them from spilling.

"Are you kidding? That one makes me want to give *myself* an erotic massage."

There was a round of laugher and one hearty "amen" to that as Jessica squeezed into the last available square inch at the wooden railing overlooking the shore.

The woman beside her—a buff blonde probably closing in on fifty with discreetly tweaked facial features—was pointing out into the water where six seriously ripped guys swam through the surf.

The view was diminished by their distance from shore, but even so, only a blind woman wouldn't feel the testosterone tide emanating from those focused, intense men swimming as if their lives depended on it.

And, of course, their lives did depend on it, since the only guys who would be out training in the middle of the ocean off Coronado Island were Navy SEALs. The shaved heads and taut, defined muscles were a sure sign the next BUD/S class must be in session. Jessica had been a San Diego resident for the past decade, and she knew even longtime local ladies never tired of catching a glimpse of the honed male perfection that went through this rigorous training.

Jess watched with detached appreciation—her work with all things sensual made her take a more clinical approach to arousal. Of course, her experience with men tended to distance her, too.

She just hoped she would bring the right mix of enthusiasm to the table tonight to present her material in a convincing manner. Stepping back from the rail, she sent a prayer off into the universe, grateful for the way the heavens must be smiling on her. She'd wanted to arouse these women with her first class on reclaiming their sensuality? Thanks to the U.S. Navy, her audience had already been majorly warmed up.

Now she simply had to divert their attention from the mouthwatering men and proceed.

"Ladies, if I can have your attention for just one hour, you'll learn the touches that will have any man begging to be in your bed."

Half the heads on the porch turned her way and two women exchanged winks.

Not satisfied with a fifty-percent success rate, Jess pressed on, determined to make this class an instant smash hit. She had an idea for parlaying one of her planned demonstrations into something that would keep this group talking for weeks.

"In fact, as a bonus for tonight only, I'll be glad to show you firsthand how these techniques play out in real life. With a real man." Capitalizing on the interest of the group, she made the most tantalizing offer she could think of. "If any one of you ladies would like to hunt us down a willing male specimen for practice, I'll demonstrate how quickly the power of touch turns any guy into a smoldering mass of muscle ready to fulfill your every last sensual wish."

A chorus of "oohs" and feminine squeals filled the balcony as the rest of the women spun away from the ocean view. And before she could consider the logistics of what she'd just proposed, two of the ladies shoved their way through their peers toward the exit.

IT HAD BEEN a long time since Ricardo—Rocco—Easton had cause to wear a bow tie. And the last time he'd donned one, the suit had been a hell of a lot more upscale than what he had on now as he worked the generic black neckwear into a knot to complete his waiter's disguise.

Still, his fingers hadn't forgotten the drill and the man in the mirror in his white shirt and tie reminded him of dress whites and—

Hell.

He turned away from the hotel bathroom mirror with an

oath, knowing he owed the bout of stupid nostalgia to this place. Coronado Island. He'd avoided this part of San Diego ever since his injury had cost him his spot among the SEALs. He couldn't even look out at the damn view from the glitzy Hotel del Coronado without a wave of memories threatening to drag him under like the surf once had along this same stretch of shore.

But for the sake of investigating the woman who had possibly scammed his car dealer father, Rocco was willing to sacrifice a few hours of mental peace.

He shoved open the bathroom door so hard it banged off the wall behind it, his thoughts of his father's failing mental health upsetting him all over again. His dad had days of clarity and days where he was more than a little muddled, so Rocco didn't know how much stock to put in his claim that he'd been swindled by a beautiful car buyer who had no intention of making a single payment on the vehicle she'd purchased from Easton Luxury Motor Cars.

Possibly his father had his facts wrong. But the preliminary paperwork backed up his statement. Jessica Winslow wasn't making her payments.

And although she was only one person—one alleged scam artist—she represented a growing new trend in deception Rocco found abhorrent. There seemed to be a rising willingness in women to use flirtation as a means to commit crime—a way to catch men off guard.

If his father had been Jessica's victim, Rocco would see she paid the dealership every cent of the loan she'd been in default on for months. The old man's business had been floundering for the past year and another bad debt could very well close his doors for good.

The injury to Anthony Easton's pride would be even more devastating than the wound to his wallet.

So tonight's mission to learn the truth was instrumental in Rocco's goal to help his father stay independent for as long as possible. And since weeding through a paper trail that might not reveal the full extent of Jessica Winslow's circumstances, Rocco's work tonight would be as up close and personal as hers promised to be, thanks to the free pass a waiter's uniform gave him around the hotel. He'd check out the woman's seminar and see for himself if she was legit.

"Oh my."

A feminine voice in the corridor ahead forced his thoughts back to the moment at hand. As he relinquished his strategic planning long enough to take stock of his surroundings, he noticed two elegantly dressed ladies frozen in the middle of the hall, matching pink drinks sloshing around their martini glasses.

At their mutual look of openmouthed surprise he was hard-pressed not to check his fly. More likely, his expression, as he thundered down the hall, had caught them off guard.

Damn it. Had his time away from the SEALs turned his covert operational skills to crap? He schooled his features into something he hoped resembled a smile.

"Ladies." He tossed in a quick bow and then realized that was something waiters only did a hundred years ago. "Can I help you find anything?"

His words broke the spell and one of them—a brunette probably nearing sixty and still smoking hot—grinned like the Cheshire cat.

"As a matter of fact…" She turned to her friend with a

raised eyebrow as if seeking approval. At the blonde's nod, the dark-haired lady continued, "We've been charged with finding a little help for a demonstration at the workshop we're attending here."

The blonde silently pointed to a door a few feet behind them before leaning in to take a sip of her neon-pink drink.

Jessica Winslow's room. Jessica Winslow's workshop. *Showtime.*

He nodded, unable to resist the lure of an open invitation into the very seminar he'd hoped to investigate. Did Ms. Winslow run a legitimate business? He'd look for the vehicle she'd defaulted on after he gathered a little intel on the woman herself. In her case, simply repossessing her SUV wouldn't bring him enough satisfaction if she'd swindled his dad.

Rocco had turned to the recovery business after his doc at a military hospital told him he'd never be fit for the teams again. While repo work wasn't exactly his lifelong dream, he'd figured he could at least help out his father by providing the old man with the service free of charge. He made money off his other clients—repossessing vehicles from deadbeat debtors. It paid the bills while he figured out what to do with his life now that he couldn't serve his country.

"I'm your waiter for the evening and I'd be happy to help." He didn't offer an arm to either woman, knowing that wouldn't be a waiter's style, but damned if the old cougars didn't each grab an elbow and cling to him like white on rice.

Not that he minded. Their friendly disposition would make it all the easier to wrangle his way into Jessica's turf. Feel out her business practices.

She'd bought an Escalade from his father's car dealership six months ago and had spent an hour in the office dishing about her work and her years in San Diego, treating the old man like a long-lost friend as she casually signed a contract she hadn't made good on. In the normal course of Rocco's business as a recovery agent—the PC term for a repo man—he would have simply repossessed the vehicle. But given that his father's personal trust had been violated by a woman who'd blatantly charmed him into not running an extra credit check, Rocco had decided to give this repossession his personal attention.

Arriving at the suite, the blonde opened the door. Rocco didn't know what to expect exactly from the title of the Winslow woman's workshop: *Better in Bed: Reclaiming Your Sensuality.* What the hell did that mean? Did she consider herself some sort of sex expert? Bad enough she'd applied feminine wiles to deceive his dad. Now she wanted to teach the art to new disciples?

Less than a dozen people sat around the spacious room as his two new female friends led him inside. The place had been redecorated like some sort of ritzy club. The normally reserved color scheme of the Hotel del Coronado had been smothered in scarlet material while white candles flickered all around. For a minute he wondered what kind of demonstration these chicks had in mind as they all stared at him. The unanimous predatory glances made him wonder if they'd been hunting for some kind of ritual sacrifice victim.

"Well done, ladies."

A woman stepped through the circle to the center of the room, her conservative black suit and messy updo in no way detracting from her blatant sex appeal.

He recognized her face—no, make that her hair and her kick-ass bod—from his father's surveillance cameras, a routine safety precaution at the dealership that had helped Rocco locate more than one debtor.

"I'm Jessica Winslow." The instructor nodded politely without offering her hand. Loose pieces of her auburn hair swayed around the chopstick device she'd used to impale some sort of twist at the back of her head. "We really appreciate you helping us out tonight for our demonstration."

Rocco had a habit of sizing up people in no time, a practice that predated his days in the Navy, although it was one that had come in handy during some tight situations overseas. But the female in front of him didn't lend herself to quick conclusions with her designer suit and her shoes, carefully polished, to hide scuff marks.

A completely remorseless defaulter would have charged new shoes while on her spending spree, so he couldn't figure out those scuffs.

"No problem. I'm Rocco Easton and—"

Whatever he was going to say died in his throat as Jessica unbuttoned her suit jacket with quick efficiency, her French-manicured fingers moving easily over flower-shaped rhinestone buttons.

What the hell? The jacket fell away to reveal a crimson-colored lace camisole that disappeared down into the waistband of her black skirt.

While a few of the women whistled as Jessica removed her jacket, she simply tossed the garment aside and wrapped a hand around his bicep. Apparently unconcerned about the eye-popping visual her breasts made in the molded lace and satin of her fitted camisole, she gestured toward a chaise longue that had been dragged into the center of the sprawling Victorian suite.

"It's a pleasure to meet you." She tugged him briskly forward, as if getting half-naked with a stranger was all in a day's work for her. "If you'll just join me right over here, Rocco, I'd like to show my guests a few instructional tips on massage."

"That's *erotic* massage, gorgeous," the brunette who'd brought him into the room stage-whispered from her post at a freestanding bar where a dozen white candles flickered. "I think you're in for a treat."

He stopped so fast, Jessica's feet stuttered as she pitched forward slightly. He steadied her automatically, his instinct to physically protect a woman—even from a stumble in high heels—overriding his personal beef with her.

The whole group went silent for a moment as if gauging his reaction. Then one woman laughed. Another snorted. And then the whole crew busted a gut over his hesitation.

Everyone but the fearless workshop leader, that is, who appeared to falter. She bit her lip with sudden indecision, a row of perfect white teeth sinking into the soft fullness of her lower lip.

"You're kidding." He didn't drop his attention from her face, but the desire to run a quick fact-gathering mission on the particulars of her body was so strong he had to take a step back.

"Are you uncomfortable being touched by a stranger, Rocco?" Her sandy eyebrows scrunched in worry over the idea.

He wondered if the moment of thoughtfulness was real or a well-acted performance. Sometimes people who preyed on others survived by developing an uncanny level of insight and empathy for the people they targeted. Was she playing him now?

"Not necessarily." He lowered his voice to slide under the cackle of excited conversation all around them. "But could you clarify what you mean by erotic massage?"

He had no intention of stripping for entertainment value tonight. Even in the headiest of his glory days with the teams, he'd never found the SEAL groupie thing appealing.

"I'm instructing them on how to give a massage that generates sexual interest, but without touching in an overtly sexual way." She proved as skilled at talking under the hubbub as him, her manner straightforward and direct in spite of conversational material that literally made the hair on the back of his neck stand on end.

And what was that about? He was here to feel out the woman's character, yet she seemed to be the one finding all his weaknesses and surprising him at every turn.

Jessica released his arm while the rest of the room quieted.

"I don't want to put you on the spot. If you'd rather not test your sensual willpower in front of a bunch of strangers, we'll certainly understand."

Possibly it was his imagination, but he could have sworn all the other women in the room leaned forward in their seats.

And he'd have to be completely lacking a pulse not to experience at least a twinge of male interest at this scenario. Even with a potential adversary doing the stroking.

But he hadn't come to Coronado Island and faced memories of his former career—the SEAL team that had been his whole life—only to get scared off by a sensual distraction. He would deal with whatever temptation lurked in Jessica's touch in order to learn more about her. He couldn't walk away until he found out if she was the kind of woman who could purposely swindle an old man.

"Not a chance." He sat down on the chaise. "I've got a good fifteen minutes before I have to get back to work. Do your worst."

2

JESSICA HELD her breath along with every other woman in the room when Rocco Easton shrugged out of his white jacket.

What was it about a set of great shoulders that commanded attention from even the most aloof feminine observer? And damn it, Jessica considered herself the queen of detached. She could provide a good deal of male testimony that would agree.

Yet something about the waiter's expressionless compliance suggested he could turn off his personal desires even faster than she could. Wasn't that an odd quality in a man who couldn't be a day over thirty? There was something strong and unyielding about him, something that reassured her he would never be overcome by an attack of lecherousness after a bit of massage.

Whatever the reason for the reserve she sensed in him, Jessica appreciated it in light of her own hang-ups.

"Well?" Rocco's voice emanated at breast level while she stood next to him.

The sound seemed to rumble right through her, sending frissons of response over her skin. And oh my, but that was an unusual reaction for her. She'd paid for every kind of counseling imaginable after the rape—well, she'd paid for it after college, during her internship at a psychologist's office, since she hadn't been able to afford it until then. Still, no amount of therapy had ever made her a wildly responsive woman in the sexual department. That coolness of her own desires had prompted her to study sensuality and make it her area of specialty in her seminars.

But being able to teach it and being able to *live* it were two different things. This waiter's ability to ignite a physical response in her so quickly surprised her more than her father's announcement, when she was twelve, that he was going to quit drinking. Of course, she figured this startling discovery would turn out to be as false as her dad's promise.

"The goal of this massage is a deep understanding of your partner along with increased physical awareness." She launched into her discussion by rote, her memorized notes coming to mind easily despite the highly unexpected circumstances of this talk.

The words made her feel in control again, arming her with much needed distance. Kneeling on the chaise beside the waiter who bore a stronger physical resemblance to the SEALs they'd seen out in the surf than to any server running around the hotel, Jessica was glad she hadn't brought a massage table. She'd wanted to give the room a suggestive ambiance instead of a classroom feel, and she thought it was the right choice, even if it made working on Rocco a little challenging.

He was built like a truck. His shoulders taxed the seams of his white cotton shirt, the V of his back tapering admirably by the time her eyes reached his belt level. If she'd seen him on the street, she would have pegged him as someone involved in physical labor. And she *definitely* would have taken note of him. No wonder her students had come in from their manhunt positively glowing with their triumph.

Rocco was a first-rate male specimen.

His icy blue eyes studied her now, his attention intense if somehow clinical. She had the impression he absorbed far more of the finer points of massage than her paying students. The eight women who were here to reclaim their sensuality all seemed to be more interested in licking their chops over their guest.

Of course, if Jessica hadn't been speaking, she might have engaged in a bit of chop licking of her own. She hadn't really missed sex in the last few years since life had closed that particular door, but that didn't mean she didn't notice men. Far from it. Her imagination had always succeeded in painting more delectable interludes with men than she'd been capable of in real life, and the stud seated to her right had the power to inspire all kinds of tasty fantasies if she had the time to indulge them.

"If you'll just turn sideways for me, Rocco, I think we're ready to begin." Jessica warned her hands not to be nervous as they fluttered over his shoulders and then landed softly on either side of his neck.

Holy Mary, Mother and Joseph.

She had to hold herself rigid in order to suppress her reaction to the electric shock that traveled through her fingers, up her arms, danced around her breasts and then seared all the way down to her womb. Did the reaction show on her face? She lost her place in her spiel for a moment as she struggled to stifle the hum of sexual energy vibrating through her now.

She peered down at her fingers, planted on his shoulders, as if she could perceive some cause for the phenomenon.

"Excuse me," she intoned finally, closing her eyes as she prayed for some memory of what the hell she'd been talking about. "I seem to have lost my place."

Rocco cranked his neck around to see her, his blue eyes sparking with the same live current she felt through her hands. She was so completely out of her depth.

"You were discussing the right times to apply a variety of strokes."

Jessica swore she could fall right into those eyes of his. They didn't appear icy anymore. The crystalline blue held a white heat that threatened to singe away all her carefully rehearsed words. Already she felt herself falling into a sea of sensations, her brain failing to grasp what strokes he was talking about.

Damn it, maybe she was *having* a stroke. Although heart failure seemed more likely with this amount of stimulation.

"Yes, Jessica," chimed in one of her students. Ingrid was a Hollywood director's wife who had driven all the way to San Diego to take the class in the hope of keeping her attendance a secret from her husband. "You were just about to show us how to caress him for maximum benefit."

The chorus of laughter began again, reminding her that she needed to keep a tight rein on the group or they would commandeer the class with racy innuendo and bawdy talk. And she had so much more to offer than that—if only she could keep her focus. She could not afford to let her unexpected reaction to Rocco derail her new business after all the years she'd worked to get this far.

"You'd just mentioned that there were different benefits

to fast and slow strokes," another woman prompted before lifting a martini to her lips.

"And could you perhaps define what you mean by 'maximum benefit' for a man? Is that a euphemism for climax?"

Damn. Damn. Damn.

"No." She raised her voice enough to drown out some other helpful soul only too happy to join the discussion. "I've remembered my place now and I'd appreciate it if you could hold your questions until the end of the session." She moved her fingers experimentally around Rocco's impressive shoulders. "I was in the midst of demonstrating the difference between a friction touch and a vibration touch. Ladies, feel free to move your chairs around or walk to this side of the room if you can't see."

As the dynamics of the group shifted and the attendees shuffled around behind her, someone knocked into Jessica just enough to press her up against Rocco.

For one breathless second, her abdomen and her pelvic bone grazed his laterals, the whipcord muscles flexing enough to provide her with an intense secret thrill.

And oh my sweet stars. She needed to focus on her job and not the ill-timed attraction. Peeling herself off him with an effort, she half wondered what he thought of her workshop. Her.

"This is the friction touch." She applied the necessary pressure, her hands ratcheting up the heat even though his skin burned beneath his shirt to start with. "It requires a more aggressive motion and it can draw your partner into a more sensual frame of mind."

She'd read as much about the massage she was licensed

to give, but she'd never experienced the magnetic pull on the other end. Not that she'd had reason to give many massages to men. She'd grown out of her old sexual fears a long time ago, but even as she'd been proud of herself for facing those fears, she hadn't exactly been wowed by sex as a college student or after. Three years after her last relationship ended, she still hadn't felt any great urge to revisit that perspective.

Until tonight.

Touching this man had her wickedly distracted as she realized she would be content for everyone else in the room to fall away. While that wouldn't be good for her business, she thought it would be deliciously good for her.

"Next is a movement called petrissage, which is a type of kneading massage." She spoke in order to help herself maintain focus, to lead herself through this lesson no matter how difficult it might be. "This technique involves light squeezing, gripping the muscles and rolling them under your hands."

Rocco's muscles were in such abundance it wasn't hard to find a sample for her demonstration.

A student nearby cleared her throat before she spoke.

"It's difficult to tell how much pressure you're applying. Do you think we might be able to talk Mr. Easton into removing his shirt? Seeing your hands directly on his skin might be more helpful."

Eight women nodded in tandem. Jessica's knees buckled just a little at the mere thought of touching Rocco's naked skin, as she noticed a tray full of scented massage oils waited nearby.

"I think we've probably detained our guest long enough

as it is." She hoped he would take the hint and sprint his sexy self right out the door before she melted all over him. "I hardly think we can ask him to—" ·

Rocco's hands were already moving over the buttons of his dress shirt, his bow tie hanging loose and undone about his neck.

"It's okay," he returned easily, his movements relaxed despite the soaring temperature of his skin. "I'm finding your workshop informative too."

And without another word, his white cotton dress shirt slithered off his shoulders, leaving Jessica facing the bronzed expanse of wide shoulders and taut sinew. From somewhere in the room, a dreamy feminine sigh seemed to encapsulate her thoughts completely.

"Maybe a little massage oil?" Ingrid said, passing her a bottle of vanilla honeysuckle blend. "It highlights the muscle groups, you know."

The wicked grin on the woman's face assured Jessica she was loving every second of class so far. Just what she wanted.

Working up her courage, she squirted some oil between her palms and rubbed them together for warmth. The scent filled the air as she lifted her hands to touch him again. Forcing her fingers onto his back, she braced herself for the electric shock all over again.

This time, her breasts ached and her breath caught. Her heart pounded so hard she feared the whole class would see the palpitations given that her camisole didn't exactly provide extensive coverage.

"This is the friction touch." She demonstrated briefly to minimize the sweet torment of caressing him. "And now we'll learn the vibration touch."

Scavenging up her autopilot teaching mode to take over, Jessica's lips moved, spouting out her lesson. But in her head, she continued to linger on the idea of a vibration touch.

Never in her life had she found a need for the battery-operated toys some women used to find pleasure. But after tonight, she would seriously investigate the options ASAP. Something about touching Rocco Easton had made her realize she would need to find a way to take the sexual edge off her thoughts or she might never think straight again.

WARDING OFF pleasure—surprisingly—wasn't all that different from warding off pain. Rocco had to mentally travel somewhere else in order to withstand the experience, his body growing more and more susceptible to its physical reactions.

Jessica's hands proved as seductive as her charm had been to his father. Rocco fell deeper under their spell the longer she talked, the longer she worked her lubricated fingers over his skin. Interestingly, the seduction didn't come from her obvious assets. She didn't employ the more expected female tactics, like brushing her half-bared breasts against his back. Instead, she simply followed the guidelines she had set out in her workshop, using her professed techniques to the letter.

There was, he thought, something honest in that at least. And he had to believe he hadn't abandoned his mission despite the way he'd allowed himself to come into such intimate contact with his investigative subject tonight. No matter what Jessica's financial picture might be, he believed she sincerely embraced the principles she taught in this workshop by the way she kept the class on track.

Not once in the half hour—he glanced at the clock—no, forty-five minutes that he'd been here had Jessica rested her fingers or deviated from what he suspected was a well-rehearsed lecture. She gave her students more information than they'd ever retain.

"Ladies, this is a good touch to use on a man's inner thigh." Jessica's words suddenly blasted their way into his consciousness, wrenching him back to the moment before he could steel himself for the impact.

A couple of the lecture attendees asked her some follow-up questions about that statement, but Rocco's brain kept envisioning Jessica applying her skillful hands to his thighs. She touched him with light surface caresses in a quick, upward movement. What would that feel like if she transplanted it somewhere more overtly sexual?

Rocco was thankful for his foresight in putting his shirt on his lap after he removed it, as his blood surged south like a rogue wave.

"What do you think, Rocco?" Jessica leaned down into his field of vision, half-bending around his shoulders to make eye contact. "The question was—which touch did you find most effective for relaxation and which for erotic purposes?"

For a minute, the words sounded like Greek, since the only language he wanted to speak was physical. He was more interested in making this woman sigh with pleasure and call out his name. He wanted to see how fast he could get her naked and have her splayed on the chaise underneath him.

Except that he wasn't here to sleep with her. He was here to investigate Jessica's character. Test the legitimacy of her business and see if it seemed to generate enough income to finance her automobile. Too bad he was too freaking distracted by the raging erection he sported to comprehend much about her other than the fact that she turned him on.

"The first touches were the most relaxing." Either that or he'd had more control early in the evening. "I think the styles of massage increased in, uh—firepower—as we went. Perhaps Jessica designed the program that way intentionally."

"And what about the scent?" another student pressed. "How did vanilla honeysuckle strike you?"

Like a freaking thunderbolt?

"Good." He nodded. "Definitely a good scent."

He looked to Jessica mostly to take some of the class scrutiny off of him. He'd never been this publicly aroused. The only time he'd been close, he'd marched his date out of the bar to take her home with him. That didn't seem like an option now.

"Where's everyone going?" He blinked his way through his turned-on state as he noticed two of the women disappearing into the connected suite.

"We've finished the erotic-massage portion of the retreat." Jessica's hand slowed on his back, her fingernails scratching lightly over his skin before coming to rest in the center of his shoulders. "A few of the women had dinner reservations downstairs they didn't want to miss, but I know they all appreciated your willingness to sit in for the demonstration."

The remaining women in the room zipped purses and jingled keys. Some moved toward the door while others checked cell phones and made calls.

One of the women paused in her conversation, and

called over to Jessica, "Don't fool yourself, hon. Those women are lighting out of here to look for men to try those massage moves for themselves. You got this class so hot and bothered I don't think anyone can face the idea of going back to their hotel room alone."

"There's a tip for you though, Rocco." The dark-haired woman who'd originally invited him in gestured to a bar glass full of cash. "We didn't want you to sacrifice any income on our behalf."

Ah crap. He'd wanted to assess Jessica Winslow's potential as a scam artist and yet the presence of the overflowing tip jar made *him* feel like the one doing the scamming.

The heaviness in his limbs made it tough to stand. The heaviness between his thighs made it a bad idea anyhow. He willed away the effects of Jessica's massage, wishing he could recover faster. He never should have allowed himself to get personally involved in the debtor's world. It was pretty much the cardinal rule of repossession work and, of course, impossible to honor if you were looking out for personal interests like his father's business. His father's pride and independence.

"The pleasure was all mine." He'd fork over the cash to the waiter who'd brought the appetizers halfway through the class. Or donate it to charity. There had to be something he could do with the cash to take away the sting of guilt. "But thanks."

The woman stepped out of the room with her friend, the silent blonde, leaving Rocco alone with his masseuse and no witnesses for all the accusations he was about to make.

As soon as he shook off this sexual spell she'd kneaded into his skin with her addictive fingertips.

"Thank you for coming tonight, Rocco." Jessica stepped back from him abruptly and reached for her suit jacket, almost as if she was nervous around him. But that couldn't be. She didn't have a clue about his real identity or his motive for being here.

What was that all about?

And moreover, how could he report back to his father on Jessica's financial standing when he hadn't done much tonight beyond finding out the woman possessed the most talented fingers imaginable? Had he gone to all the trouble to drive into San Diego and remember all he'd left behind on Coronado Island only to go home with a damned inconvenient hard-on to show for it?

Hell no. He hadn't become a repo man for the fun of it. He'd done it to help out his father's failing business. So he'd damn well do his job tonight, even if it meant confronting Jessica to find out the truth.

His plan for the night might have been delayed, but it was far from over. As an ex-SEAL, he was pretty good at assessing a situation and adapting as the need arose. He also knew better than to have any qualms about confronting a woman on her perfidy. He'd backed away from it once before and the end result had forced him out of the military for good.

"I didn't come here just to work at your retreat." He needed to remind himself of that fact—he'd gotten entirely too caught up in everything Jessica was selling.

Still, he couldn't help but hope he'd been wrong about her. Or rather, that his father had been wrong about her.

"Really?" Her eyes widened as she shrugged into her conservative black jacket and covered up the fire-engine-red camisole. "You came here for something else?"

She tipped her head sideways, her eyes wide as her fingers froze above the unfastened jacket buttons, her silver bracelet jingling gently.

And then she took a step toward him. He was still on the chaise longue and finally had himself under control again. The moment seemed surreal after she'd been so careful to keep physical distance during the massage. Her hands might have been turning him inside out with expert touches, but she hadn't ever stepped over the line into sexual teasing or flirtation.

He didn't think it was conceited of him to suspect that had taken some restraint on her part. The chemistry between them had been as irrefutable as the heat still rolling off his body and the jump in his pulse whenever she touched him. That chemistry simmered all over again now as she sank to sit beside him on the chaise, her hip just inches from his.

Anger churned beneath the heat. Anger at himself for being drawn in by her, and at her for attracting him in spite of a formidable willpower that had successfully hauled him through weeks of training that pummeled and defeated ninety percent of the guys who attempted it.

Damn it, he missed life as a SEAL, where the line between right and wrong had been more clearly defined, determined by the military or at least by his team as a group. Now he forged his own path. Was forced to trust only his gut without the resources of the Navy at his fingertips or the support of his team to back him up.

"I came here to—"

Investigate you.

But the words remained unspoken in the face of her expression. There was an openness about it, a yearning that was so palpable it seemed almost innocent.

Her gaze flicked down to his mouth, her pupils dilated. *She wanted him.* She thought he was a damned waiter and she wanted him.

Not exactly the behavior of the gold-digging schemer he'd expected.

"Yes?" she prodded, nipping her lip and spinning her silver bracelet around one wrist while she waited for him to explain why else he had come to the workshop.

Shit.

Was she more innocent than he'd believed? Could she have gotten in over her head with her credit because she was naive or had somehow fallen on hard times? The memory of shoe polish covering the scuff marks on her heels nipped at his brain. The need to find out the truth weighed on him, forcing him to wait a little longer. To see what else he might learn about her.

Then again, maybe he just needed an excuse to taste her. To test the level of her innocence for himself before he confronted her with the reality of her bad debt.

Taking what her eyes had offered him long ago, Rocco slid his hand around the back of her neck to steady her and drew her closer. Her eyelids fell to half-mast, then drifted closed. He couldn't have stopped himself if his father had launched the surveillance videotape at his nose.

Shoving aside second thoughts, he pulled Jessica's mouth to his and kissed her.

3

THE EFFECT PROVED more potent than alcohol.

Jessica no longer wanted that chardonnay she'd longed for before the workshop. Rocco's kiss made her head spin. The soaring sweetness soothed any hesitation she'd had about taking a seat here next to him in the first place.

She'd been right to want this.

She *needed* this.

For too long she'd shied away from intimacy. First out of fear; later, out of fear of disappointment that she'd studied sensuality in every conceivable form and still wouldn't be able to relax and let go.

But this kiss told her that had been totally unfounded. Nothing about Rocco disappointed. He tasted as good as he felt, his lips covering hers with a gentleness that stunned her coming from such a powerful man.

Heat fanned high inside her. His mouth moved over hers with a skill that turned her inside out. He tilted her chin up, and her mouth opened to him without any conscious decision on her part.

His tongue stroked hers, coaxing a sigh from deep in her throat. She wanted to sink into the moment, to stop every clock for an hour—a day, maybe—to savor each conceivable nuance. As it was, sensations bombarded her, dragging her into a sea so thick with longing she couldn't imagine how she would ever surface.

"Jess." He whispered her name over her lips between kisses and seemed to urge her body toward him.

Not until then did she realize how perfectly still she sat beside him, only daring to give up her mouth to this man. Old habits were hard to break, but heaven help her, with Rocco, she could see herself making a good dent in her hang-ups.

Inching closer to him, she followed the soft pressure of his hand sliding down her shoulder to the small of her back. She nudged her left breast against him and she hesitated for just a second, testing the feel of it and discovering the touch lit up her insides. Pleasure coursed through her, flooding every nerve ending and urging her to seal her whole body against the fiery heat of his.

All of it was new to her. The immersion. The joy of it. The sense of wanting the kiss to go on forever. She'd always been painfully aware in every encounter she'd ever had with a man, second-guessing every awkward moment.

Regardless of how gentle he was, she appreciated that he didn't roll her beneath him, Now, lying by his side, she had access to his bare chest.

At almost the same moment she laid a hand on his side, he speared his fingers beneath the jacket she'd never buttoned. He stroked the silky camisole, his hands skimming up her sides until he cupped the undersides of her breasts.

Oh.

The feather-light touch held impossibly devastating consequences. She wore nothing beneath the camisole, the silky fabric providing her last line of defense against the touch that would conquer her completely. She knew it from the way her nipples beaded in anticipation.

He broke the kiss to study her, his blue eyes dark as a turbulent sea. She fell into that swirling chaos, her breath dragging through her lungs with labored effort.

How could she have worked so hard for years to rid herself of sexual difficulties while this man could stride into her life and swipe them away with one incredible kiss?

His thumb stretched over the cup of her camisole to tease the bare skin of her exposed cleavage, his caress patient and thorough. She breathed in his scent, clean and spicy at the same time. The light from the flickering candelabra cast his face in shadows that alternated with a golden warmth.

She wanted this, wanted him, with a hunger that shocked her. Her whole body trembled in breathless anticipation for what would come next. She wanted to be naked with him, burning with him, following this inferno wherever it would lead.

"Damn it."

He swore softly as his hands vanished from her body with no warning.

"What?" Confused, she tried to read his expression. "I bet there are condoms at the gift store."

She'd shop personally if he wanted her to. She wouldn't let anything come between her and—

"No." He shifted positions, sitting up on the chaise until his feet hit the floor at one end. "I didn't mean for this to happen."

Confusion swirled through her as she tried to make sense of what he was saying.

"But I wanted you, too." And wasn't mutual consent a beautiful thing? She knew what she'd been feeling hadn't been one-sided. "I've never felt like—"

"Don't." He swung on her, that one word a barked command. "Just—don't."

He turned away from her to reach for his shirt and all the frustration and anger she'd ever felt about intimacy suddenly simmered hot in her veins. How come sex could never work out for her? She thought she'd been so close this time. Kissing Rocco had been the most physically transporting experience of her whole life. And he had turned away from her as if nothing had happened.

"I don't understand." She stood, the tremors of desire that had lit her insides just a moment ago turning to resentment and embarrassment. "If I did something wrong I damn well deserve to know."

Even if that served to increase her embarrassment. She refused to be kept in the dark over what had gone off course this time. She'd battled too hard for some semblance of sexual well-being to let this guy tear her down.

Standing, he buttoned his shirt as they faced off across the chaise.

"You want to know what went wrong?" He scooped his tie off the floor and wrapped it around the neck of his half-open shirt.

"Please." Her whole body vibrated with thwarted longing, her cheeks flaming hot along with every other square inch of her skin.

"I'm not a waiter."

Did he think she would care about his career? Was he embarrassed about his job?

"It doesn't matter to me what you do for a living." Heaven knows, she hadn't exactly strolled out of a middle-class upbringing. She'd gone to bed hungry too many times as a child to ever disrespect what someone did to earn a living. She would have given anything for her father to hold down a job for more than a few weeks at a time. Maybe then she wouldn't have ended up in foster care by the time she was a teen.

Maybe she wouldn't have been assaulted because no one was there to help her navigate the confusing waters of sexual relationships.

"You don't understand. I'm a recovery agent."

"A what?" She was still trying to figure out what his job had to do with not wanting her.

"A repo man."

The words possessed a sting she hadn't expected. After all, more than a decade had passed since she'd put the fears of her childhood behind her. There had been a time when *recovery* agents, as he called them, had held a hell of a lot of power over her life, thanks to her derelict parents.

But not anymore.

She waited for him to explain himself, her gut twisting with new foreboding.

"I came here tonight purposely to investigate you and see if you were the kind of person who could lie to an old man's face in order to drive away with an upscale new car." His eyes turned icy blue again. "I needed to find out if that beautiful body of yours housed the cold heart of a first-rate scam artist."

HE'D ENVISIONED this moment in his head more than a few times. He'd played it over and over since learning the father who'd raised him single-handedly was in deep financial trouble and that Jessica's ploy might be the straw to break the camel's back.

But not once had he envisioned the sputtering disbelief—no, make that fury—on her face.

"What kind of sick joke is this?" She actually trembled with anger, her shoulders shaking with it, and he wondered if he could be missing some piece of the puzzle. She didn't seem like the kind of woman to play on an old man's sympathies, but damn it, the Escalade he'd seen in the parking lot told him she didn't mind reaping the benefits of her deeds.

"It's no joke." He reached in his pants pocket for his business license, regretting he'd let things get so far out of hand. He'd overestimated his willpower when he had allowed her to massage him, a mistake that had made it impossible not to kiss her. He'd avoided relationships since his accident, a conscious choice since he hadn't been fit company for anyone with the anger and resentment weighing bitterly on him at all times.

But, of course, that meant he'd avoided sex, too.

Touching Jessica had been too much, too soon after a celibate stretch. His blood still pounded so heavily through his veins he swore he could hear a percussion section jamming in his head.

"Of course it's a joke," she spit back at him, yanking the chopstick device out of her hair until the auburn waves tumbled freely to bounce on her shoulders. "Either that or you're the sorriest excuse for a repo man I've ever met. I have credit card statements that show my payments for the last six months. For that matter, I have the most recent printout in my vehicle. We can retrieve it before I let the security guards all over this hotel know that you've been harassing me."

"A bill can't always be considered proof." No doubt she had a house full of bills if she was the kind of person who defaulted on her purchases. "I'd need proof those bills were paid. And the finance company says they haven't been."

"I haven't even received a late notice." Her voice pitched higher, her frustration level revving up fast for someone he'd suspected of being a smooth operator. From the surveillance tape footage, he'd suspected her game would be tight. But right now she didn't appear to have much experience scamming anyone. Damn it, he'd approached this thing all wrong. He was better at covert operations, staying behind the scenes and only moving in at night under the cover of dark. That strategy had been his go-to move as a SEAL and it was a strength he'd carried into the repo business. Why couldn't he have stuck with what he did best?

The answer came to him instantly. He'd messed up because this had been personal. His father had been stressed and Rocco had wanted to clear it all up as fast as possible.

"Look. I'm sorry that I let things get personal." He'd been an idiot to kiss her, even if it was proving damn tough to regret it. "I planned to come in here and get a feel for what kind of person you are—"

The whole situation sounded ludicrous, all the more so because he'd let himself touch her. Taste her. Want her in spite of everything.

"So help me, if you had dared to make any false accusations in front of my hard-earned clients, I would have sued your sorry ass for everything you're worth." She stomped across the floor to retrieve his white jacket and tossed it at him. "In fact, why don't you give me the name of your company and your supervisor and I'll make sure that person knows how close you came to landing your company in court tonight."

A thread of unease tickled his instincts. Either she was a hell of an actress, or he'd wronged her in a big way.

"I saw you on the surveillance tape from my father's dealership." He spoke more to himself than to her, going over the evidence in his mind.

But what had he really seen? A black-and-white tape of a woman who looked like Jessica from a foot or two above eye level. A woman with her body. Her hair. And of course, her car.

Ah, shit. All at once it occurred to him that after his preliminary viewing of the tape, he'd handed the case over to his new assistant investigator to do the legwork. Rocco had wanted to move on it quickly and he'd been tied up with other business. Could the other investigator have overlooked something obvious?

"I'm waiting." She had retrieved the pad of hotel stationery from a small desk and stood with pen poised above it.

Frustration hummed like a deerfly around his head at the possibility that someone at his company hadn't triple-checked their paperwork. In the Navy, his buddies had always backed him up, but in the outside world, good backup wasn't a given. Yet another aspect of how life as a civilian sucked.

"I need to check the VIN number on your vehicle." He set his jacket back down on the chaise, knowing he wouldn't be satisfied until he saw some proof of Jessica's alleged fraud for himself.

"Excuse me?" The glare she sent him would have withered a lesser man. "*I'm* the one entitled to information here and I'll be damned if I let you wiggle your way out of it."

Okay, he resented the image of himself wiggling. After all, he hadn't hurt her—he'd kissed her, for Chrissake.

"I work for myself. *I'm* the company. Sue me." He removed a business card from his wallet and slapped it on the minibar. "Now I'm going to check out the VIN on the Escalade and see if you have a legitimate beef before we take this discussion any further."

He had an extra set of keys in his pocket. He didn't need her permission to check out a vehicle he was here to take into custody anyway.

Unless, of course, it was a different vehicle.

Anger flared hot inside him as he opened the door into the hall. He'd been overwhelmed with new cases this past week and he'd given a higher priority to firming up new accounts than taking care of detail work on recoveries in process.

"Where do you think you're going?" Jessica had set down her pen and paper before following him into the quiet corridor. "You're not touching my vehicle without my permission."

"You can sue me for that, too. First I'm going to find out if there's been some kind of mistake and we've got the wrong vehicle."

He'd owe her one monster of an apology if that was the case. Except he'd seen the security tape of her buying the car. It had looked just like her, damn it. Same killer body. Same sexy-as-hell red hair. Even the same mannerisms, right down to a little habit she had of spinning her bracelet around her wrist.

"Of course you're wrong." She hastened her step, her sweetly endowed form jiggling enticingly with the effort.

Why the hell couldn't he keep his eyes in his head around her?

He pushed the elevator button to go down to the main floor, intrigued in spite of himself at how quickly she'd transformed from a reserved professional to a hot-blooded lover and then to a spitting-mad, in-your-face, woman as tough as any debtor who'd ever followed his tow truck into the night while shaking a fist.

Now, she gave him a wary glance before stepping into the elevator with him. Folding her arms, she managed to cover only a small portion of her considerable personal assets.

"So what's a vin and why didn't you look at it before you attempted to humiliate a taxpaying entrepreneur struggling to make ends meet?"

"Vehicle Identification Number. It's etched into the dashboard under the windshield of every vehicle made and each one's unique. Like a Social Security number for cars." The elevator door opened and he stepped off onto the main floor of the famous Victorian-era hotel. "And I didn't try to humiliate you."

It was just that he'd been stressed about his father for months. His dad had taken it to heart when Rocco got a medical discharge and he'd been trying to compensate for the letdown by starting a business that could help the old man. But maybe he'd been so focused on making it up to his father that he'd unwittingly hurt someone else.

The exit was mere steps away and he plowed through it, slowing only to hold the door for Jessica. As much as he hated to be wrong in life, this was one time when he sincerely hoped he'd screwed up. He didn't want this woman to be a scam artist.

The attraction he'd felt for her had been strong. Immediate. Undeniable. To have those feelings for someone totally lacking in scruples…

Hell. He wouldn't appreciate what that said about him.

"It's over there." Jessica pointed out the massive vehicle spit-shined to gleaming perfection before she smiled at a security guard striding through the parking lot. "And I'm only following you to gloat about this when you find out you're wrong."

Her high heels tapped a fast pace, making him realize she needed to take two steps to his one to keep up.

"If I'm wrong—" he dug the paperwork on the vehicle out of his wallet and unfolded it "—you're going to have a whole world of new problems to worry about. You can forget about gloating."

The tap, tap of her high heels slowed. Stopped.

"What do you mean?" Her perfume—no, the scent of her soap—rode the breeze off the ocean, winding around him as he compared the digits on the paper to the ones under the windshield.

They didn't match.

He didn't know whether to thank God or curse himself. No doubt a little of both was in order. Still, he hadn't been kidding about this situation only getting more difficult for Jessica.

"I mean you've got a woman impersonating you and using your name on a car loan and who knows what else." Though he hated for her sake that this had happened, he couldn't help his relief that she wasn't a scam artist.

"You still think there's another vehicle with this number you have that's somehow associated with my name?" The professional woman was back, her brow scrunched as she tried to make sense of the situation.

A situation she didn't deserve to be in and one he would damn well help her resolve since he'd only added to her trouble.

"Yes. There's another Escalade purchased under your name by someone who looks a hell of a lot like you and who's obviously using all your credit information. I'd say you've been a victim of identity theft by somebody who knows you very, very well."

4

"DAD?"

Rocco dropped into his bed late that night, exhausted but knowing he wouldn't sleep until he'd told his father the news. Moonlight streamed over the bed. He'd never bothered to hang blinds, living out in the middle of nowhere had its advantages.

He just hoped his dad was having a good day and would remember what Rocco was talking about with the Escalade. The old man's health had been slipping lately, but his doctor didn't think it was Alzheimer's. Yet. Still, Rocco noticed gaps in his father's memory and he worried about doing any kind of work that would make him less accessible when his dad needed something. At least now, as his own boss, he had the freedom to drop everything and lend a hand at Easton Luxury Motor Cars or help his father out at home if he needed anything.

"Ricardo, why do you call me so late?" His father's accent became stronger when he was tired. He'd come over from the old country in the sixties, but being in the States for forty years hadn't smoothed the strains of Italy from his speech. "I have to work tomorrow."

Rocco closed his eyes as he laid his head on the pillow

and tried not to think of Jessica Winslow's massaging fingers on his shoulders.

"I know, Dad, but you made me promise I'd call when I found out anything about the woman who hasn't made payments on her Escalade." It was because his father had been so upset about it that Rocco had jumped into his investigative efforts without doing his homework. From now on, he needed to remember his father's condition could make him more emotional. Less logical. But damn it, that hurt to think about. His father had always been so strong.

"You found the redhead and my car?"

"I found out the redhead was impersonating the real Jessica Winslow and that Ms. Winslow is the victim of identity theft, so I'll have to do some more digging to find out who really has the Escalade."

His father cursed in Italian and then in English for good measure.

"They try to break an old man's bank, but thank goodness, my son, he is too smart for them, no?" Anthony Easton sighed into the phone and Rocco could picture his father lying back down in his bed. "You're a good boy, Giuseppe, you know that?"

A lump stuck in Rocco's throat. Giuseppe was his father's first son by another marriage—a son who'd died in a car accident on a California interstate years ago. A son his father never would have mistaken him for unless he was sliding deeper into dementia.

Or perhaps he was just tired.

"It's Rocco, Dad. And I'll let you know when I find the Escalade, okay?"

With a soft grunt, his father seemed to agree before he

hung up the phone. Leaving Rocco alone with his worries for the man who'd raised him and a renewed determination to find the woman who had ripped him off.

He just hoped Jessica Winslow didn't spit in his face the next time she saw him, because he had the feeling he was going to need her help if he wanted to catch the redhead who'd faked her way into a brand-new SUV.

BUMPING AND GRINDING to the wail of Hindi sitar music the next morning, Jessica led the day's first workshop in the hotel's double suite. She tried to tune out the hum of anxiety that wove through her head louder than the stringed melody.

A fruitless endeavor.

She'd barely slept the night before, spending hours on the phone trying to find real live people at her credit card companies to report the case of identity theft. The police hadn't been much help, assuring her she needed to follow the official channels set up by the credit bureaus first before they could get involved.

Eventually, they'd admitted they might be able to help her if she brought them a tape of someone impersonating her in order to secure a car loan. Even so, she needed to contact the finance company first.

And, of course, the mere act of talking to the police set her nerves on edge. She'd had too many run-ins with the cops in her childhood to feel any sort of ease in that situation. Even though she didn't have anything to hide these days—unlike in the past when she'd been forced to make up long, convoluted explanations for why there had been yelling coming from their apartment or why her parents hadn't registered her for school in their newest hometown—she still felt tongue-tied and anxious when she tried to recite her story. While part of her couldn't help feeling a twinge of resentment at Rocco for bringing all this to her doorstep, she knew she should be grateful that he'd alerted her to the identity theft. She'd had a few instances of bills not showing up and a handful of purchases on her credit card that weren't hers and which she'd disputed with her company, but nothing she'd worried about until now.

Still, she definitely nursed more feelings for Rocco than simple gratitude. She couldn't deny the twinge of hurt she'd experienced that he'd turned away from their heated kisses so easily. She hated that she'd thought about those moments so often through the night, but that revelation of sensual potential inside her had been as big of news to her as any identity theft.

Between the lack of sleep, financial worries and a body overwrought by desire for a man she should probably stay away from, she wasn't exactly bringing her A game to the morning belly-dancing class. Securing the good opinion of these students should be her number-one priority.

Like that of the woman tentatively raising her hand…

"How do you recommend we incorporate this into our seduction techniques?" asked the quiet blonde who had been the first to arrive for today's workshop.

The woman, Bryanna, was best friends with the Holly-wood director's wife, and had confided to Jessica this morning that she feared her husband was on the verge of asking for a divorce.

Jessica weighed her answer as she helped one of the other ladies find the rhythm of the music by gently steering her hips.

"I don't recommend using this to seduce anyone but

yourself." She spoke from her heart, knowing the answer probably wasn't what the woman wanted to hear, but hoping the message would make sense anyway.

"How can I seduce myself when it's *me* who notices all the cellulite every time I contract my stomach muscles?" Bryanna slowed her undulating movements, her harem-girl dancing costume not as sheer as some the other women had chosen.

Jessica wasn't sure if she should play it safe and make a few suggestions for setting the stage for seduction, or if she should forge ahead with what she really thought. Bad advice could cost her that coveted word-of-mouth business. But damn it, she had to trust her gut on this.

"The dance is meant to help you see beyond the superficial of the exterior so you can feel the sensuality of the movement and tap into a new wellspring of sexual confidence and well-being." It might sound New Agey, but the approach had worked wonders for Jessica when she'd been at her most sensually vulnerable.

Other students slowed their dance movements to listen, the flow of sheer silk skirts and scarves coming to a halt.

"What good is reclaiming my sexuality if I don't have anyone to share it with?" Bryanna straightened, her body rigid with tension Jessica could feel from several feet away.

Or maybe Jessica simply recalled too well what it felt like to experience self-doubt after her own sexual confidence had been scared into hiding.

"Tapping into your own sensual power creates an aura of attractiveness and charisma that draws people, without any effort at all from you." No seduction necessary.

At that moment, someone rapped on the door to the

connecting suites where they conducted their workshops. One of the students in back moved to admit the newcomer. The door frame filled with shoulders and one-hundred-percent he-man.

Rocco Easton.

Feminine squeals greeted his arrival as if he was some sort of rock star. Clearly he had created quite a following for himself with his fake persona of sexy waiter. Would these women still admire him if they knew his true identity or that he'd bluffed his way into their midst the night before?

She couldn't imagine what he wanted anyway. Hadn't he screwed up her life enough already? Or did he want to embarrass her after all and snatch the keys to her car in front of her whole class? Still, the sight of him in khakis and a navy polo shirt that showed off amazing muscles elicited a purely feminine flutter inside her.

"Rocco, darling." Ingrid, the director's wife, drew him deeper into the room. "We need you to settle a friendly disagreement we've been having this morning about the nature of attractiveness."

"If this is about lipstick color or something, I'm not going to be much help." He sauntered inside, his eyes meeting hers. Holding.

Jessica's skin tickled with the memory of his touch, her heart picking up speed at just the sight of him. She might have doubts about his motives, but she didn't doubt their sensual connection for a second. And she didn't want any part of that sinfully sweet reaction.

He was a repo man, a guy who sneaked onto people's property at night to make off with the cars that struggling families depended on. He was the guy who told lies to latchkey kids about why he needed to take away a refrigerator housing nothing more than milk and a few precious eggs.

"We aren't discussing cosmetics." She couldn't keep the frosty tone from her voice, most of her anger self-directed for her unwanted response to him. "I am trying to explain that I think a lot of a person's attractiveness comes from a certain self-confidence—"

"Sexual self-confidence," Ingrid clarified, shooting a meaningful look at her friend, who'd raised the whole question.

The Indian music wailed to a halt, the CD turning itself quietly off while Jessica wondered how she'd ever get the class back on track. Bad enough one of her students was taking the workshop during what was obviously a dark time in her life, but why did Rocco have to return in the midst of her morning session?

"Self-confidence—sexual or otherwise—is hot as hell." Rocco jumped directly into the conversation as if he had every right to be there. "Women want men who have it and men want women who have it."

"I thought men liked to be needed?" Bryanna waved a yellow scarf around with an exasperated flap of her arm. "Am I the only one who thought men like to feel needed?"

She turned to the other women in the class, a couple of whom shrugged while others nodded. Jingling ankle bracelets and tiny fingertip bells chimed discordantly.

For a second, Jessica felt grateful to have the question directed toward their male interloper. She wasn't so sure she'd want to tackle it in front of a roomful of women more savvy about men than she was.

Rocco shook his head as he kept his eyes on the woman asking the question.

"Men like to be needed to change a lightbulb or play small-time mechanic, but they don't want to feel responsible for someone else's happiness. And personally, I think the guys who do get off on that kind of power trip grow tired of it in a hurry." Shrugging, he turned to Jessica, clearly unaware of how keenly he'd probably just pegged Bryanna's husband. "I came to see when you would be free today. I need to speak with you as soon as possible."

The intentness of his stare seemed to untie a ribbon within her, unfurling a billowing swell of want.

Could the whole room see her reaction? Her cheeks burned at the thought of how close she'd come to falling under the spell of a man who'd thought the worst of her just twenty-four hours ago.

"I'm in the middle of a workshop." She wagged her dancing scarf as proof. "I'll be tied up until noon."

He checked his watch and then glanced about the room at her students. "Would you mind if I stick around until you finish?"

Jessica couldn't have contradicted the chorus of affirmatives if she'd tried. The man had earned himself a full-fledged cheering section simply by being a fine-looking male.

Okay, better than fine. Still. She couldn't create the right environment to look inward and find sexual confidence if every class involved the watchful eyes of a handsome man. No doubt some of the women would strive to seek his approval, then—

"Unless that's not okay with your instructor?" Rocco had turned to her, holding off until she gave the okay.

As if she had a choice.

Gritting her teeth against her frustration and awareness, Jessica nodded.

"It would be our pleasure to have you, if you'll just stand to the side while we practice our next dance." She moved to the CD player, expecting to be obeyed and steeling herself to his presence. She'd never get through the hypnotic Dance of the Seven Scarves unless she could tamp down this fire inside her and find her teaching mode again.

Ingrid patted his arm as he walked past her, and Jessica wondered if women touched him all the time just because he looked like he would feel so damn good.

She knew firsthand just *how* good.

"Ladies." She waved her scarf in the air to regroup and attract their attention. "I'm going to show you some of the basic steps, but first I want to discuss what is so sexy about belly dancing."

"The outfits," Ingrid blurted, never requiring an invitation to contribute.

Bryanna raised her hand briefly with a waggle of manicured fingers before taking a guess.

"It's the original striptease, right?"

"No, although that's a commonly held misconception. The origins of the dance are much more tame and it's only been in the last two centuries that Westerners have put this spin on the movements." Jessica had enjoyed every second of the belly dancing classes she'd taken in college in the hope of accepting her own body again. She'd been in a dark place emotionally, and her instructor had treated her like a favored daughter, teaching her the philosophy as well as the steps.

She owed so much to so many people who had touched

her life once she'd finally broken free of the foster-care system and wasn't required to have any contact with her birth family again. She had healed in so many ways.

"Then why do you think it's sexy?" another student asked, sending a veil over her shoulder with a flounce.

"It awakens the sex chakra, *muladhara*." She rotated her hips, the sheer dancing skirt over her leggings brushing her thighs with a feathery caress the cotton tights didn't mask. "Heat is generated in the midsection that acts as a physical stimulus for the dancer and a visual stimulus for the viewer."

She didn't mean to lock eyes with Rocco at that moment. The gesture could probably be considered flirting and she didn't want to flirt with him. But the heat stirred by her slow undulations flared all the warmer for his eyes on her.

"So if you could follow me." She lifted a scarf in her hand and made a swooping motion with it, sailing the silk through the air. "We'll step forward and bring the feet together, then swipe the veil across the body like so."

Jessica wove through the dancers, helping the students emulate the moves she'd been taught as a student. Keeping her eyes on the other women in the room helped her restrain herself from dancing in front of the sole male guest whose presence she didn't forget for a second.

"Like this, Jessica?" Bryanna called to her from the end of the line, her veils twisting around her shoulder as she spun.

Something about her body language shouted a frustration she didn't voice.

"A little looser, maybe. Have fun with it." Jessica reached to steer the other woman's shoulders, shaking them gently.

"If the dance is for me, what does it matter what it looks like?"

Jessica felt the woman's pain as keenly as if it were her own. She recognized Bryanna's disconnection with her body, remembered the secret shame of having no interest in sex in a world that glamorized the carnal at every turn.

"You need to see the beauty in your sensuality more than anyone else. It's important to take the time to make the dance special for you." Jessica hadn't allotted a "getting to know you" time in the early half of the workshop, hoping to introduce her students to the classes as a warm-up to sharing their reasons for coming to the retreat. But maybe that had been a mistake since Bryanna, at least, seemed to need more discussion before she would be able to see the value of what they were doing.

The idea bothered her and she debated rearranging the retreat schedule to accommodate the need, except that trying to cram more into the day meant less time for untangling her financial problems. Less time to shore up a business that might be crumbling under her feet without her knowledge if she was developing bad credit.

The worries stressed her out until she simply turned up the music and danced with her students, gratefully losing herself in the slow grind of hips and the aching call of the Indian guitar.

She danced until the sex chakra burned and the mental tensions melted away beneath purely physical sensations. Her students seemed to have fun, and by the end of the session, even Bryanna seemed to be enjoying herself as she danced with a veil that Ingrid tied over her eyes. The hour had passed quickly.

The students filed out of the room with a caterer who would lead them to their lunch on the hotel's Windsor

Lawn overlooking the ocean. Leaving Jessica sexually keyed up and alone with Rocco again.

Coincidence?

The thumping of her heart suggested otherwise.

Still, she wouldn't give in to base urges just because she was glad to have finally recovered those urges. The universe had a damned funny way of putting a woman on the spot sometimes.

"I'm sorry to have disrupted your class, but it's important I speak to you." Rocco didn't waste a breath. He closed the door behind the last of her workshop attendees and turned to face her. "I want to help you get to the bottom of the identity theft and I have a few leads that might help."

He stuffed his hands in his pockets, making her realize she'd been staring at them. Fantasizing about them on her body.

"I don't want any help from a man who came here thinking of the worst of me." She needed distance from him, not help. She grabbed a floor-length silk robe and flung it over her shoulders even though her outfit wasn't all that revealing.

The more layers, the better.

He eyed her silently, his square jaw flexing.

"Don't you at least want to know what I found out?" He sauntered closer, bringing the scent of aftershave into sniffing distance of a woman already hypersensitive to his presence.

To back up a step would make her appear intimidated. Or worse, as though she was somehow admitting the attraction. Sexual energy crackled inside her, concentrated between her hips.

"Why should I trust anything you have to say?" She kept

her tone straightforward despite her anger; giving in to an emotional rant would serve no purpose. She regretted raising her voice and cursing the night before. She'd worked too hard to remold herself for a setback to reveal her roots so quickly… "You purposely deceived me yesterday, letting me think you were someone you are not. You know what they say—fool me once, shame on you. Fool me twice…"

"I want to help you." He brushed her shoulder, the barest of conciliatory gestures, and she stiffened.

Her automatic defenses kicked in when the innocuous touch threatened to melt her knees.

"You don't even know me." Although he did know how she liked to be stroked. Kissed.

More heat swelled. She needed to get out of here. Away from him before she wound up caving in to desire.

Then again, was this just another means of pushing away the possibility of sex? She'd become adept at avoiding intimacy for most of her adult life, and now, the one time she felt something wildly exciting with a man, was she just jumping at any excuse not to feel that way again?

Sometimes having a degree in psychology provided her with *way* too much self-knowledge.

"It doesn't sit well with me that I jumped to conclusions about you." He released her shoulder, his hand disappearing from her body. "I didn't do my homework where you were concerned and I nearly sabotaged the wrong woman's business reputation. For me to say I'm sorry isn't adequate."

Jessica listened but heard his words only peripherally. Her mind kept spinning with tempting images of indulging her desire for Rocco. Wasn't that the next logical step in her personal healing journey? Now that she'd reclaimed her sexuality through years of workshops and study, she ought to master it. Flex it when she wanted, and ignore it when she was ready to move on.

Right now, heaven help her, she wanted to flex it with Rocco. As an expert in repossessions and as a man who must have some experience with identity theft, she'd be foolish to push away his help. And as a woman who was more than a little attracted to him, she planned to follow that chemistry wherever it might lead—at least long enough to find out how freeing sex with a man like Rocco Easton could be.

ROCCO HAD NEVER met such a difficult woman to read. And that was saying something since he'd gone head to head with a lady spy during a critical overseas mission and had been sucked in like a schoolkid.

But at least with that particular sexpot traitor he'd figured her out sooner rather than later. Thank you, God. With Jessica, he still couldn't get a handle on her.

She could be so aloof sometimes, like when she was teaching and she avoided his gaze even though he couldn't take his eyes off her. Last night she'd been able to teach a class while he'd been struggling to ignore a chemistry that had his eyes crossing and his tongue dragging. Even now in the vacated double suite where she'd danced with her students just moments ago, she seemed a million miles away, oblivious to the effect her sensual movements had on him.

He'd been lucky to survive belly dancing class. Every red blood cell had cruised south so fast he'd damn near fallen over. But he'd remained here, determined to right this wrong he'd done to her. He might not be saving the world anymore, but he could still make sure this woman got a fair shake from life before he walked away.

"So what do you say?" He nudged her finally, unable to wait any longer, while she stared off into space with the dreamy expression of a woman who knows a juicy secret and won't share.

"Hmm?" Her dark eyes shifted his way and she seemed to become aware of him for the first time since she'd dismissed her students.

"Will you let me help you?" He allowed his gaze to roam down her veils where they hooked on one shoulder. The view there seemed safer than if he took a visual inventory of the sexy indent of her waist through the robe.

"Definitely." Her decisiveness surprised him as much as the decision itself.

No arguments?

No caveats?

She really was different from any other woman he'd ever met.

He reached into his pants pocket to retrieve the mini storage drive with the saved surveillance file on it, but Jessica distracted him by turning around and standing with her back to him.

"You can start by helping me take this off." Sweeping her long auburn hair aside, she exposed the buttons that held the halter top of her dance outfit together.

She dropped a veil that had been draped around her shoulders, exposing the vulnerable line of her spine disappearing into the low back of her top. He could reach out and trace each vertebra along that patch of bare skin.

"I'm confused." His voice sounded just like it had in the

weeks after an enemy had attempted to strangle him during a covert rescue mission.

Raspy. Dry. For totally different reasons.

"What's not to get?" She half turned to look at him over one shoulder, her eyebrows arched in curious surprise. "You want to help me to reach some kind of personal absolution and I can't unhook those fastenings without some serious contortions."

He weighed that explanation like a hostile negotiation. He knew if he didn't pay close attention he'd miss something important.

"I thought you wanted to sue my sorry ass." He put his fingers on the dark buttons hidden against the dark fabric. Her clothes carried her warmth, her scent.

He resisted the urge to lean into her hair and inhale the fruity smell of her shampoo, but he couldn't stop himself from running a finger along the inside of her collar, down one side of her neck.

"I was angry last night and I think I had good reason." She tilted her head to one side, giving him all the more room to explore her creamy skin.

And only then did his sex-fogged brain start receiving the message. She wanted him. No matter that he'd falsely accused her the night before. She stood here before him now, back arched like a cat, her hips mere inches from his, asking him to help her undress.

He'd barely been able to resist her yesterday when he'd still had reason to think she'd scammed his father. What the hell was going to hold him back now when he'd thought about her all night long, dreamed of her peeling off her clothes and offering herself to him.

His eyes flicked toward the exit, assuring him the last of her students had already left. With the self-locking doors in the hotel, only someone with a key could come in.

He didn't stand a chance now if she wanted to finish what they'd started the night before.

"You don't seem angry today." He didn't wade in foreign waters without making every effort to know what lurked beneath the surface.

His close call with the female spy—the whole reason behind the injury that had cast him his spot with the SEALs—had assured him he had zero judgment when it came to women. It was tough to shake that kind of wariness even if he didn't believe she was some Mata Hari in search of secrets.

He undid the first button.

She stilled.

Then her breath hitched. "When you kissed me last night, was that part of your plan to find out what kind of person I am?"

His fingers stalled on their path up her throat.

"Never." It had occurred to him afterward that he had set a new personal record for rule breaking in crossing the line with Jessica.

He'd wanted a less structured lifestyle when he left the navy and he'd found it in repo work, but even then, he tried to stick to some basic guidelines for recoveries. Not getting personally involved topped his list.

"So it's not like you kissed me out of spite. There must have been something else at work to make you kiss a woman you wanted to dislike."

She reached back to the narrow placket of buttons

behind her neck and unfastened the last one. Her top slithered down her body until she caught the fabric to her chest.

She turned to face him, the tops of her breasts visible over the knot of fabric she clutched in one hand. He didn't speak and it was no wonder—his brain had stopped working a long time ago.

Women had thrown themselves at him in the past, SEAL groupies out to bang one of the Navy's elite. Jessica struck him as different. He wasn't sure how, but he could see the difference between her and someone like the woman who'd convinced him to be a demo subject for the workshop. Despite Jessica's provocative area of expertise, she wasn't an overt flirt. There was a quiet reserve in her and a steely strength he'd glimpsed when she'd railed at him over his mistake with the Escalade that held a unique appeal.

Besides, Jessica wanted him now, when for all she knew he'd never been anything but a repo man. She wasn't trying to seduce him for the charge of being with a SEAL.

"If you're not going to help me undress, maybe you'd better go so I can change out of my dance clothes." She winked as she gestured vaguely toward the door.

Dismissing him.

Like hell. He was so turned-on he was scared to move for fear of jumping her. He would be coming off the longest dry spell of his adult life, after all.

"It's your fault I can't get my head together." He didn't leave. He just watched her. Waited to touch her until he could be sure he wouldn't move too fast. Scare her away.

"How do you figure?" She slipped off her high-heeled shoes and stood in her bare feet on the thick carpet.

"I can't stop thinking about your dance. The way you

moved your hips." He stepped closer, swiping aside her discarded shoes with his foot. "I just keep wondering if you've
ever tried those kinds of rotations with a man seated deep
inside you."

5

HER HEARTBEAT REVERBERATED through Rocco's fingertips as he absorbed the pounding of her pulse at the base of her throat.

He'd taken the game up a level, and he wasn't sure if she was comfortable with the new stakes, but he'd bet his whole company that she was as turned-on right now as he was. He wanted to get to know Jessica Winslow and he could see it wouldn't happen if they circled around each other, talking and pretending to be people they weren't. One night with her would teach him so much more, so much faster. He would know her from the inside out. Now that he didn't have any SEAL secrets to guard anymore, he had the freedom to do that.

Besides, this was a woman in touch with herself—a woman without a bunch of emotional baggage he couldn't handle. No way in hell would he get wrapped up with a woman he might hurt out of his own emotional inadequacy.

She never did respond to his murmured comment. She simply arched up on her toes and pressed her lips to his. Petal soft and lipstick sweet, the kiss remained tame for all of two seconds. Then she let go of her halter top and wound her arms around his neck, skimming her naked breasts over his chest.

The contact erased all reservations. Sensations bombarded him, coming at him from every angle. The flowery scent of her filled his nostrils while his hands roamed over her body. He wrapped his arms around her, his fingers taking in the silky smooth texture of her skin and the voluptuous curves of generous hips and breasts. Her auburn hair flowed over his arms, thick and fragrant.

She drew on his tongue, overt and provocative as if she couldn't push things fast enough. Apparently she'd gotten over any embarrassment at his sexual suggestion since she strained against him, wiggling her leggings off her hips in a dance hotter than any of the practiced moves he'd seen from her earlier.

The rocking rhythm of her disrobing nudged his erection relentlessly, seductively. He broke the kiss to grind his teeth and hang on for dear life.

"Wait." He gripped her hips, holding her steady for a few precious seconds until he got himself under control again.

"What?" Dazed, she stared at him in confusion, her dark eyes not completely focused. "Too many clothes?"

She reached for his belt while her dance outfit peeled down another inch on its own. Her breasts had been bare beneath the dance unitard, but she wore a black cotton thong beneath the leggings. Pink rhinestones outlined a heart on one hip.

"I want to see you. Feel every inch of you." He'd ached all night with the want of her combined with guilt for what he'd done. Now he wanted to soothe that need for both of them. "I didn't get to touch you last night the way you touched me."

Her breasts swayed as she shifted, allowing her leggings to fall away from her thighs and pool at her feet.

"I—" She stepped from her outfit, her teeth worrying her lower lip with small nips. "I thought you would be pleased to have a woman so hot for you."

Her fingers stilled on his belt, her cool skin tantalizing against his hot flesh.

"I'm crazy about it." Insane was more like it. "But I'm not going to be selfish. Just because you're the reigning authority on sensuality doesn't mean I'm going to rake in all the benefits without giving back."

She nodded vaguely and he used the moment to scoop her up off the floor and into his arms. She squealed in surprise as he charged toward the connecting bedroom in the hotel suite.

"You don't have to—"

"I want to." The guttural plea came from somewhere deep inside him and he knew he'd let her get too close to him. "I have to."

The bedroom was dark, the blinds still drawn and the bed neatly made. He dropped her into the middle of the simple white coverlet, her auburn hair spilling over the bedspread like a red wave.

She was so freaking beautiful. Her abs contracted in a flat plane that disappeared into the waistband of her panties. The pink rhinestones winked at him in the half-light, taunting him into removing her last scrap of clothing.

Fire blazed through him, creeping up his back and branding his thighs. He covered her, savoring the feel of her on every possible square inch of his skin.

"I'm going to take such good care of you." His thigh fell between hers and he steadied her legs with his hands. Need moved from an ache to a raging inferno and he wondered how he'd ever keep it in check.

Bending his head to her breasts, he tongued the tight tips, circling and laving until she arched beneath him. A small cry issued from her throat, an urgent hum he couldn't answer yet. Not if he wanted to show her even a fraction of the pleasure she'd given him yesterday with nothing more than her hands.

"You said yesterday that your massage techniques would work on a man's thighs." He skimmed his hand down her curves to the front of her leg. "How about a woman's?"

Spreading his fingers wide, he spanned her flesh to apply the technique he'd learned yesterday. Slow and kneading at first, then increasing in pace and friction.

Her eyes opened wide for a moment, their gazes meeting in recognition of the touch. The intent.

A flash of worry raced through her expression for one moment, a hesitance he hadn't expected when she'd all but stripped for him.

He must have imagined it. Forgetting about what he'd seen, he edged higher up her thigh, closer to the source of her heat. Her hips bucked and she gripped his forearm with one hand as if she could steer him or forestall him— he wasn't sure which.

Sealing her mouth to his, he kissed her at the same time he peeled away her panties. Sweat beaded along his back from the restraint, but he would pay her back in full for the free instruction she'd given him yesterday and for her forgiveness today.

"Come for me." He whispered the words onto her damp lips as he eased a finger inside her.

She went unnaturally still. Holding herself back, or—

Finding her release.

She writhed beneath him, hips twisting and thighs

squeezing against the pressure of his touch. The convulsions pulsed along his finger and his palm, surprising him with their strength.

Her eyes fluttered open with a wonder he hadn't expected, a surprised joy that didn't mesh with how much sexual experience she must have to give extremely expensive workshops on the subject.

Maybe he was just that good.

Grinning in spite of himself, Rocco released her to unfasten his pants. He couldn't wait another second to lose himself in her, to reap every lush, sensual reward of her obvious pleasure.

"Wait."

Her hand squeezed his forearm again. Tighter. More urgent.

He glanced up to see that worried expression lodged in her eyes; this time, there was no denying it.

"What's the matter?" He'd fix it regardless of where it came from. If she wanted lime-green condoms or some kinky new massage oil or for him to chase her naked around the room, he would make it happen.

"Can I be on top?" Her eyes darted from side to side and he realized he might have put too much weight on her. He'd been a 225-pound wall of muscle in his SEAL heyday, but even after his time on the outside he'd probably only lost about ten pounds of that.

"Anything." He rolled off her, taking her with him so that she straddled him.

His pants had only made it to half-mast, but he wasn't picky. He'd make love to this woman with his shorts around his ankles any day of the week.

"I—" She still looked panicked, even with her cheeks flushed from the orgasm he knew damn well he'd given her. "I'm worried my students will be knocking on the door any minute for the afternoon session."

Her thighs tightened against his, her whole body stiffening.

"I'll put out the Do Not Disturb sign." He plucked her off him and slid her aside to do just that. He'd forgotten about her workshop.

"But—" She quieted when he walked out into the living area of the suite to hang the sign and, as an added precaution, pull the security lock into place. He ditched the rest of his clothes on the way back. Yet by the time he returned, she was out of bed with a sheet wrapped around her like a shawl, pacing the floor.

"Did I miss something here?" He paused in the threshold, wondering what the hell had happened to the woman who'd been tearing his clothes off with frenzied hands.

He throbbed for her and she seemed to be plotting an escape from bed.

"No." She stopped her pacing and shook her head. "That was the best, the most incredible—I just wonder if we could finish this later."

Perhaps she read some of his dumbfounded shock in his expression because she hurried to clarify.

"Just until after today's workshop sessions. I can't afford to have my students banging on the door and wondering where I am."

Her grip tightened on the sheet and he couldn't shake the sense that she was worried. Panicked. Almost as if—

"Jesus. You're married, aren't you?" His gaze flew to her ring finger for a telltale cheater's tan line.

"No." She shook her head, denying it adamantly as her red hair flew around her shoulders. "Of course not. I just don't want to mess up my class and—"

"And you think this is going to send your students running if they find out I spent your lunch hour with you." He believed her about not being married, spotting no evidence of a wedding ring and having researched her background when he thought she was in default on the vehicle loan.

But obviously, she was a more complicated female than he'd thought. He needed distance to get his head together and figure out what to do next.

He reached for his clothes, seeing that arguing with her would be pointless. He'd be lucky if he could even zip up without taking his skin off, but he'd be damned if he'd beg for sex.

"I'm sorry." Her words sounded sincere enough, but he didn't put any faith in his judgment. After all, he'd been wrong about everything when it came to this woman.

He retrieved his pants from the other room and found his shirt there too. She followed him, her bare feet silent on the carpet while her sheet trailed behind her. Getting his ass back on track to find her identity thief would be a good way to distract himself right now.

"I've got a lead on the location of the woman who's using your identity and I'm headed out there this evening if you want to go." His words might be terse, but he was frustrated as hell right now. He didn't particularly look forward to a reunion if it meant more of her game playing, but he wouldn't feel better about the accusations he'd made to her face until he attempted to help her with the identity theft problem she was facing.

For all he knew, maybe her hot and cold attitude today had been her brand of revenge after he'd falsely lambasted her yesterday.

"Rocco, I didn't mean to—"

"I've got some business over at the base this afternoon, but I'll be in the lobby at six if you want to track your identity thief." He was too frustrated to hear her out and too edgy to be nice about it. "Enjoy your class."

Sliding across the security lock, he opened the door and let it swing shut with a satisfying slam.

"HAVE YOU SEEN ROCCO?"

Just when Jessica thought she'd escaped the afternoon session of her workshop, Bryanna's voice pulled her back to the quickly emptying meeting area. The talks had gone well enough, considering the obvious pitfalls of discussing Kama Sutra positions in a public venue. There had been plenty of sex jokes, moments of embarrassment, and the revelation that one woman had never had an orgasm.

But none of those challenges compared to the well of dread that pooled in her belly at the mention of Rocco's name.

"Not since this morning." She pasted on a smile and put her feet back in gear, eager to return to her room so she could figure out how to fix things with Rocco and ponder the sex issues she obviously hadn't fully healed.

"Did you know he's really a recovery agent?" Bryanna gathered up the stack of reading material that Jessica had given out as part of the retreat. "A repo man?"

That got her attention. Had his motive for being here—his intent to repossess her Escalade—leaked out even after he'd realized his mistake?

"Really?" Jessica hated to lie outright so she hedged instead. "Did he tell you that?"

"No." Bryanna hugged the books to her chest, her tennis bracelet sparkling in the soft light of the table lamp. "Ingrid heard from one of the waitresses that he wasn't a waiter but a repo man and a former SEAL."

She might as well have said the guy was a rock star. All of San Diego loved their SEALs, the women especially.

So who would leave one of the military's most elite divisions to run a recovery service? The former seemed so honorable, the latter so incredibly…distasteful.

"A lot of guys claim to be ex-SEALs, you know. It's a chick magnet." Although, heaven knows Rocco had the body to back up the claim. Most of the repo men from her past came with more of a beer gut than a six-pack.

Jessica had been light-headed with lust just from looking at him. She still couldn't believe she'd freaked out when he had been about to consummate things. She'd wanted to, dear God, she'd wanted to. But when he'd been on top, she'd had a flashback to being held down in the back of Scott Baylock's car, her mouth covered by his hands as he stole from her everything she wouldn't give him willingly.

She blinked briefly, locking that memory away where she didn't have to think about it.

"There's a Web site where you can look up any guy who's ever been a SEAL," Bryanna continued, straightening an emerald-cut ruby on a chain around her neck.

"Ingrid checked it out during lunch and Rocco was totally on it. He's the real deal for sure."

She sounded so certain that Jessica figured it was probably true. Ingrid seemed like a woman who'd know about that type of Web site. What did that mean if Rocco was a former SEAL? Who went into repo work after making it through the rigors of SEAL qualification? Did he have a good reason for omitting that part of his past?

Considering her childhood, Jessica certainly understood taking liberties with one's personal history, but it made her all the more curious about the man.

"Ah." She didn't know what to say, unsure what Bryanna wanted. "Well, I haven't seen him since lunch and I'd better let you get to your spa appointment so you can enjoy the final phase of the retreat tonight."

The women would all receive luxury treatments in the hotel spa. Jessica would have attended with them if she wasn't so rattled over her near miss with Rocco and the realization that she hadn't recovered her sexual well-being after all.

"Oh. Okay. But if you see him, feel free to give him my number." Bryanna withdrew a card from one of the books in her pile. "I'm sure I'll be single within the next few months and my husband would choke on his own jealousy if I dated a SEAL."

Bryanna's grin seemed so genuine and heartfelt that Jessica didn't know what to say. Of all the classes she'd attended this weekend on reclaiming her sensuality, nothing had cheered Bryanna as much as the thought of simply sleeping with a gorgeous stranger.

Why couldn't Jessica take equal pleasure in something so elemental? She thought she'd worked through all old reasons for avoiding sex, but the old ghosts had sacked her like a rookie quarterback, leaving her dazed and confused and deeply regretting what had happened with Rocco earlier.

Even more disheartened than before, Jessica took the woman's number and headed for her hotel room now that her workshop was over for the weekend. Attendees would spend the night in the hotel to take advantage of the spa facet of the weekend, but she was finished teaching.

It had gone well enough, even though she'd been distracted by the events of her personal life. She thought she'd covered her butt with a great wrap-up discussion that had solidified her relationships with the women who'd attended.

She didn't think she would be able to make any progress with her credit fraud problems on a Saturday, but she could at least research her options a little more thoroughly. Unlike Rocco, she didn't know much of anything about identity theft other than what she'd gleaned from a few childhood neighbors who haunted local garbage cans for Social Security numbers to sell.

If she could assess the problem, she could figure out a plan for damage control once she knew how much her finances had been compromised. The hit to her personal accounts were bad enough, but a black mark on her business credit...

She had everything she owned tied up in Up Close and Personal because she believed in the concept wholeheartedly. Too bad she couldn't retreat from her own life for a little while.

Her phone rang before she reached the elevators, distracting her from the pity party she desperately wanted to throw. She didn't recognize the local number but hoped there might be a credit fraud representative on the line returning her call.

"Hello?"

"Jess?"

Rocco's voice reached right through the phone and sent a pleasurable shiver through her, followed by the realization that she should be completely embarrassed to talk to him again after the way she'd frozen up before.

"Yes. Um…hi."

"Is your workshop finished?"

She ducked into an empty corner near a house phone and a stand full of tourist information.

"We just broke for dinner a little while ago." She hadn't given him her cell number, but perhaps his call had been forwarded by her business number. "My clients will remain at the hotel for some other services, but my work here is done."

More likely, he simply knew far too much about her.

"My meeting at the base ran long, but I'm ready to scope out the lead I have for the woman who impersonated you at my father's dealership."

"Shouldn't we just turn the information over to the police?" She didn't know if the woman could be dangerous and she certainly didn't have a clue what exactly was involved in "scoping out" a criminal.

"You're welcome to pass along the information, but since my main concern is to retrieve the Escalade this woman has essentially hijacked, I'm well within my legal rights to seek out the whereabouts of the vehicle."

Strains from a piano playing nearby filled the silence and she couldn't help but wish she could just lose herself in the elegant world the Hotel del Coronado represented.

She'd had high hopes for her first big retreat and maybe just a little false expectation that by teaching her workshops to an exclusive clientele she would somehow fall into their ranks.

The notion struck her as all the more naïve—and far from her reality—now that her credit might be going down the toilet because some ballsy stranger was impersonating her.

"You might be well within your rights because of your business, but I don't know what I would do with that kind of information besides pass it on to the police."

"No problem. I'll leave a note for you at the hotel desk tomorrow if the lead pans out and I find the woman who did this. I just thought you might have a personal interest in seeing who knows so much about you that she's passing herself off as Jessica Winslow all over town." In the background of his call, she heard him switch up the volume on the music he'd been listening to, some kind of samba-mambo type. "Good luck with straightening everything out, Jess."

All at once she realized he was about to write off her and her indecisiveness. By leaving an impersonal note with a desk clerk tomorrow he was effectively shutting down communications with her and ending whatever connection they'd shared.

And as much as the spark of intimacy freaked her out, she knew that kind of chemistry didn't happen with very many guys. Actually, it had never happened with any other guy. Besides, a gun-shy girl could do worse than an ex-SEAL for an experimental sex encounter. Didn't military men come with at least a small amount of insurance that they weren't felons or lunatics?

"Wait." She pivoted in the hall. Headed back toward the lobby. "On second thought, I do have a personal interest in this."

And you.

"You want to go with me?"

She couldn't decide if he sounded surprised or—alarmed.

"I think we have a lot of unfinished business between us."

His silence suggested he'd been prepared to walk away for good. The Latin music filled the airwaves for a long moment before he spoke again.

"I can be in front of the hotel in ten minutes."

6

"SOUNDS LIKE a booty call in the making."

Lazarmos "Flare" Reverchon pounded back the last of his ginger ale outside the Blue Fin bar while Rocco whistled for his dogs. The pair of white Akitas ran out of the surf and up the beach past the outdoor tables where the late-afternoon lunch crowd had blended seamlessly into happy hour.

"I wish." Rocco opened the dogs' cages in his truck bed and the two bounded in, always ready for a ride.

Even if he wasn't.

How would he handle the twenty-minute drive with Jessica sending out do-me signals in the seat beside him when he knew perfectly well her sexual interest could turn on a dime?

Lazarmos scratched Maggie's ear before snapping the cage shut.

"Yeah? Don't the women go for pickup trucks and junkyard dogs like they go for Navy tattoos?" Laz flexed a bicep, generating a hum of feminine appreciation from a throng of women heading to happy hour.

"If you're asking if I've managed to get laid since my discharge, the answer is none of your damn business. And

I don't think Scrapper appreciates the junkyard comment." He raised the tailgate on the barking dogs. "I do repo work, not trash pickup. Big difference."

"So seriously, who's the chick that wants you at her hotel in ten?" Laz glanced from Rocco to the admiring women who flirted with him all the way to their surfside table.

"I tried to repossess her vehicle when she was the rightful owner." Rocco swung himself up into the gray Ford's cab. "Needless to say, she was a tad pissed. I'm trying to help her figure out who took her ID."

"The gentleman's way into her pants."

Rocco started the truck. "Have I told lately to go to hell? You'll be one sorry-ass SEAL when the Navy spits you out like the bad seed you are and you've pissed me off too many times for me to do you any favors. I might have found a place for you in the fast-paced world of repo work." He backed out of his parking spot, his elbow hanging out the window as he cranked the wheel.

"You're fantasizing big-time, man," Laz shouted over the noise of Rocco's engine as he revved it into Drive. "When me and Uncle Sam part ways, I'm retiring to the beach. The last thing you'll catch me doing is holing up on some spread in Dulzura with no water in sight. It's unnatural!"

Yeah, right. Rocco burned rubber on his way out, answering his first diving partner with high octane and bad attitude, two commodities Laz had always understood.

Rocco knew his former teammates didn't understand his total retreat from all things military, but they'd never been escorted out of a naval hospital because they were too weak to walk alone. And none of them had ever opened discharge papers that booted him out on his ass faster than God had evicted the first residents of paradise.

Flying down the coast of Coronado, Rocco thought about Laz's real reason for wanting to see him today. Rocco's old friend had a cop brother who'd risen high in the San Diego PD ranks and Laz wanted Rocco to use the connection and sign on for law enforcement. The conversation had been a repeat of one they'd had when Rocco started up his recovery agency, but a life with a badge didn't appeal to him any more now than it had back then.

Of all people, Laz ought to appreciate that. His nickname, Flare, came from Laz's refusal to call for help no matter what the circumstances. No red flare distress signal would ever be lit by that man. Stubborn as hell and twice as proud, Laz was the last guy to suggest bringing in backup, so Rocco didn't know why he'd be so quick to offer it.

Pulling into the Hotel del Coronado's main driveway, he put away his personal frustrations and tried to focus on a game plan for dealing with San Diego's local sexpert, the oh-so-sexy ice princess Jessica Winslow.

She was standing out on the curb near the hotel, a leather briefcase under one arm and a life-size male torso under the other.

"I don't think I have room for your friend," he called out through the passenger-side window as she approached the truck.

Her nose crinkled in confusion before she glanced down at her side and seemed to become aware of her anatomically unfortunate companion. The torso was missing everything from the waist down.

"He doesn't take up much room." She pulled open the

door before he could get out to play gentleman. "Thanks for the ride."

"I was surprised you wanted to go." He'd been prepared to write off their odd relationship, reasonably certain she'd gotten big-time cold feet where he was concerned. But he couldn't deny the rush of relief he'd experienced when she agreed to come with him today.

Clearly, the male-dummy-toting sex queen had affected him more than he cared to admit. Still, he planned to play things a little safer with her from now on.

"I surprised myself." She tossed her legless friend in the jump seat and climbed in beside him, her mid-thigh skirt riding up just enough to make his mouth water.

"What made you change your mind?" He pressed the gas as soon as her seat belt was buckled, needing to set this trip in motion. His reserves around her were going to be limited no matter how much he lectured himself about the perils of lusting after a sexually indecisive woman.

And how weird was that?

She taught sensuality and sex etiquette to the rest of the world and didn't have a clue what she wanted in bed for herself.

"For starters, I realized I can't afford to take risks with my business credit and I'm beginning to think you're right about it being difficult to obtain help straightening out an identity-theft problem." She tucked her briefcase under her seat and turned toward him, knees together.

As he pulled up to a stoplight, his eyes went back to her skirt hem, focusing on the fabric stretched taut above her thighs. If he had X-ray vision, he would start his visual journey right there.

"But that's just for starters?" He wanted to hear her other reasons, her personal incentives to spend more time with him.

"I thought it would be good for me to take a few chances." She folded her hands on her lap, seemingly aware of where his eyes wanted to be even when he was watching the road.

"Okay, explain this to me. You're comfortable with carting male dolls around town and giving workshops on sexual assertiveness, but you think you're not taking enough chances in life?" He drove east, away from the water, and couldn't deny a sense of relaxation coming over him as he left the remnants of his old world behind him. Again.

He didn't want to think about a future as a cop or the fact that his teammates thought he wasn't making use of his skills as a repo man. His old man had been singing the same song for months. The only thing that interested Rocco now was Jessica, and she did a mighty fine job of monopolizing his thoughts.

"First of all, I don't teach sexual assertiveness so much as comfort with sensuality, but that's another story. Second, I don't mind taking chances on a business level. It's my personal life that tends to go dormant if I don't force myself to—" she sent him a sideways glance that he felt more than saw "—mix it up now and then."

She'd revealed more about herself in those two statements than he'd managed to intuit in the past twenty-four hours.

"It seems that you'd have to be fairly bold on a personal level to rope strange men into massage demonstrations, but that's just me." He wanted to quiz her about the distinction between sexual assertiveness and sexual comfort, a difference that seemed important to her somehow, but he wasn't sure how to frame the question without it taking on intimate overtones given what they'd shared.

Or rather, *almost* shared.

And how was it they wound up talking about sex when he needed to back off this relationship?

"You know how some professional entertainers adopt a stage personality for performing?" She smoothed the hem of her yellow skirt stitched with butterflies, a far cry from the belly-dancing outfit she'd worn earlier in the day.

Still, Jessica made butterflies seductive.

"You mean like strippers called Vanessa Vamp or Betty the Body?" He knew a few far more colorful names but didn't think he should spout them now when he was trying not to think about sex. He would fix this woman's problem and move on with a clear conscience.

"Not quite." Frowning, she shifted her knees away from him to face the windshield. "I was thinking more along the lines of concert performers who use visualization to imagine they are world-renowned divas and gain confidence by adopting that facade. Only, in my case, I adopt the facade of an unflappable massage teacher I once had who could lead couples touch therapy without showing the least hint that anything they did turned her on."

He was so speechless at the image her words planted in his mind that a mile passed—or ten—before he got his tongue working.

"You attended couples touch therapy?" He couldn't help a wave of rogue jealousy toward the guy who'd introduced Jessica to this kind of stuff. How many men could talk their girlfriend into learning naked sex massages? Then again, he might have imagined the naked part. Still…

He adjusted the AC vent to blow right into his face. If he thought the airflow would reach his lap, he might have tried that instead.

"No. I attended massage therapy alone so that I could offer sessions on massage during my workshops for Up Close and Personal. Then after I worked with the teacher for a while I became her apprentice for six weeks and followed her into some of her more unorthodox sessions."

"So you emulate this woman in your own classes." He steered the conversation back to safer terrain, unwilling to endure a twenty-minute drive sexually aroused.

"It helps me find the necessary separation from my subject matter so I don't start thinking inappropriate thoughts." She pressed the button to roll down the window, allowing the breeze to blow through her hair.

The auburn strands danced along the back of the seat, lifting away from her neck to reveal the slender column of her throat. Damn it, why couldn't he keep his eyes on the road?

He needed a conversational about-face right now before he drowned in hot thoughts about her.

"How long have you been in business for yourself?" Teaching erotic massage and Seduction 101.

He didn't stand a chance of steering this discussion into safe terrain when even her job centered around sex. Passing a slow-moving car, he took out his thwarted hunger on the accelerator.

"Six months." She tucked a flying lock of hair behind her ear, revealing thin gold hoops in side-by-side piercings. "I celebrated my first round of workshops by buying the Escalade. Not that I personally need a lot of brand names in my life, but I thought my clientele would expect a certain image from their sensuality expert. The field is sort of delicate, you know? A sensuality expert who shows up in a leather miniskirt and a Trans Am is viewed as a tramp. But if I arrive in linen and driving an Escalade…"

"Ah. Kind of like a repo men driving a souped-up truck with a rifle rack in the back." He didn't plan to use any of his firearms but, like her, he preferred to work with people's expectations instead of fighting the stereotype.

"Exactly. Although rumor has it you used to travel with a Navy ship and diving equipment."

He did not want to go there today. Not now. Not with her. Laz had already made him feel like enough of a sellout without her jumping on the bandwagon.

He'd just as soon subject himself to her hot and cold sex drive, where he at least had a fifty percent chance of feeling good about himself.

"Maybe so. But I don't think either one of my occupations provide half as much conversational interest as the local sex authority." He'd wade right into dangerous territory if it meant leaving his past behind. "Tell me, Jess, how did you get to be such an expert on all things sensual?"

THE HOT LOOK Rocco slanted her way sent feel-good endorphins pinwheeling through Jessica's whole body. If he had stopped the truck, she would have let him have his way with her on the front seat at the side of the highway.

As it was, Rocco kept driving while she struggled for air and a scrap of brainpower that wasn't tied up imagining him pulling her clothes off.

"I'm no expert." If she was, she would know how to turn

the sensual tables and seduce him as easily as he'd undone her this morning.

"Your business suggests otherwise."

He downshifted as he exited the highway on the south side of town. The weather remained clean and bright here, unlike the changeable coastal areas where mist and fog warred all day with the sun. Still, the setting wasn't half as upscale as the hotel they'd left. The streets were in transition, with small, older homes butting up against audacious new construction swarming with contractors' trucks. The neighborhood didn't look much different from Jessica's home on the north side of San Diego where she'd felt lucky to snag one of the run-down older places in a neighborhood about to explode in value.

Her parents' lack of intelligent consumership had inspired her to study those kinds of patterns so she could reap the best rewards with what little she had in life. She'd won a scholarship to attend college for free and had earned a small wage working in the campus counseling office on weeknights. She'd proved to herself that you could come from nothing and make something out of it—contrary to what her mother had groused about all her life. Her mother had been depressed about Jessica's father's drinking and hadn't seen a way out of their unhappiness or her poverty.

"No. My business suggests I can help people get in touch with their sensuality. That's not saying I can hand anyone the keys to sexual mastery. I just help people find new comfort with their sensual selves."

"Your retreat this weekend was called Better in Bed."

"But I'm helping people to *feel* better in bed, not necessarily how to *be* better. You see what I mean?"

He navigated the truck past a drive-through burger joint and around a park where young moms pushed strollers next to teenagers playing pickup basketball. The scent of hot pavement and cut grass drifted in through her window.

"You started a business to help people feel comfortable with sex." Rocco pulled over on a street behind a wallpaper outlet. "Actually, that might explain a lot of things."

He put the truck in Park and swung around in the seat to face her. His eyes darkened as he watched her, and she had the sense that he looked right through her.

"Good." She nodded absently, feeling her confidence ebb the same way it had evaporated this morning when he'd covered her. "Now that we've cleared up that matter, can you tell me where we should be looking for this woman? A dead ringer for me, right?"

She surveyed the surrounding street, hoping he'd just change the subject. As much as she wanted to take this relationship further—if only because he was the first man to seriously turn her on in years—Jessica wouldn't let him dig through her past as part of the bargain.

"Are you uncomfortable with sex?" He caught her hand and held it.

If he'd touched any more of her than that she might have shut down completely. Heaven help her, she did have personal space issues—even with the hottest guy imaginable.

But Rocco was smart in ways she hadn't predicted and he kept his touch light. Easy. Nonthreatening.

"What makes you think that?" Was there a chink in her hard-won armor that he could see through her so easily?

"Something went wrong today when we were together and I don't know what it was. Things were great one minute and the next you iced me out so fast I got freezer burn on my ass."

His thumb smoothed up the pulsing vein in her wrist, the nervous jump of her heart painfully obvious as she struggled with a comeback. Should she admit to her sexual hang-ups or let him think she was the world's biggest tease?

"I'm sorry about that." Her cheeks heated at the memory of precisely how good he'd been to her. "And actually, I do have a few *small* bedroom issues that led me to develop the sensuality retreats in the first place."

He waited, his thumb circling around and around the inside of her forearm, the gentle touch entirely at odds with his imposing presence and the guns stacked behind them.

Clearly, he would have liked to understand her better. Or maybe he just hoped to pave the way to another hotel-room encounter. Either way, Jessica didn't have any intention of opening her past for public viewing. The reality of what that would mean helped her look beyond the magnetic draw of Rocco's seductively light touch. She wanted another chance with him, but not if it meant trotting out her issues for his inspection.

"Do you see her?" Breaking the moment, Jessica peered down the street in search of her impersonator, but she didn't see any redheaded women or black Escalades. "Do you think she works around here or lives nearby?"

His hand vanished from her skin, leaving her to wonder how she'd ever seduce him back into her bed while pushing him away at the same time. Now there was a subject for her next workshop.

"The woman we're looking for gave a cell phone

number on her loan application and the bill for that phone comes here—1233 Parkway."

He pointed to a small house not all that different from the one Jessica owned. The compact ranch-style structure had probably been built in the sixties, with a poured concrete patio by the front door. There was no deck furniture or decoration on the door, and nothing about the residence communicated anything about the owner. Even the blinds were drawn so she couldn't see if there was furniture or people inside.

"You think the woman who stole my identity could live here?" She strained her neck to see around to the back of the residence.

"Maybe. Although this could be the home of a friend or relative who collects mail for her. But I looked up the address in a reverse phone directory and there's no land line associated with this place. It's a rental unit that's been let to a small corporation for a little over a year." He stretched his legs and eased back his seat as if settling in for a stakeout.

"How did you find out all this?" She studied him with new interest and maybe a little wariness. "I didn't think recovery agents were supposed to be able to access so much private information."

"Yeah?" He grinned, looking thoroughly pleased with himself. "Maybe I do a better job than your average repo guy."

"We had a repo guy break into our house one night and steal the TV." She'd cried for days over the loss of Saturday-morning cartoons, the high point of her childhood for the two months that her father had managed to hold on to the television.

"Technically it wasn't stealing if a recovery agency was brought in, but they're not supposed to enter a locked property."

Bitterness filled her throat. "They're not always terribly ethical, you know?"

Those cartoons had drowned out the hungover fights her parents had been too drunk to have the night before. And the fact that the repo guy could steal things in the night had increased Jessica's growing sense of insecurity in a world pretty freaking scary to begin with.

Rocco didn't respond and she wondered if he would try to defend the slippery ethics of his work. But when she turned to face him, he simply pointed out the window behind her head.

"I think this is our target to your right." He whistled softly under his breath. "And damned if she doesn't look just like you."

7

IT WASN'T the first time someone had told Jessica she looked like Leslie Ann James. The woman Rocco pointed out on the Chula Vista Street was no thief, however.

"I know her." A surge of relief flooded her as she realized there must have been some kind of mix-up. "She was my next-door neighbor when I was placed with a foster family back in Colorado. We roomed together my first year of college."

Jessica reached for the door handle, ready to say hello and straighten out the misunderstanding. She didn't know how Leslie Ann's paperwork could have crossed paths with hers, but obviously there'd been a mistake.

"Hold on." Rocco restrained her, his big arms wrapping around hers to prevent her from opening the door.

She waited for the fear to come, the heartsick lurch in her gut that she experienced whenever she was afraid of being overpowered. Strangely, there was no stomach-churning anxiety. Instead, she felt only awareness of him and curiosity about why he'd prevent her from speaking to Leslie Ann.

"But she's an old friend. You must have the wrong—"

"Look." His word whispered over her ear as his finger

pointed past Leslie Ann toward the house she'd just exited. "See what's in the garage back there?"

Tearing her attention away from the redhead who used to be a blonde but had always borne a strong resemblance to her, Jessica peered at the dilapidated structure in the backyard of 1233 Parkway.

"What?" She couldn't see anything in the garage because it was closed. In fact, nothing at all struck her as unusual, other than the fact that her old friend stood a half block away and Rocco didn't want her to acknowledge the woman.

Just before Leslie Ann disappeared around a corner, she pulled out a cell phone and started to dial. With her hair colored that shade of red, she really did look a lot like Jessica.

"Check out the view in the window." Rocco released her slowly, his hands easing away even though his chest stayed close behind her.

"It's an Escalade, isn't it?" She could make out the black paint and a hint of the windshield shape.

"You bet it is. I'm going to see if I can get in there to crosscheck the VIN."

He shoved open the driver-side door.

"No." She lifted the handle on her side of the truck too. "There must be a reasonable explanation."

Feet hitting the pavement, Jess hurried in Leslie Ann's direction.

"What are you doing?" Rocco shouted to her, but she ignored him, desperate to talk to the woman who'd vanished from her life after their year as dorm mates. The streets were hardly crowded in Chula Vista's quiet urban sprawl, but the woman could duck into any of the shops or the cars parked along the curb if Jessica didn't hurry to catch up to her.

"Leslie Ann!" Jessica hollered through cupped hands, hoping the sound would travel far enough to make her quarry turn around.

She reached the corner and spotted her walking away. Calling out her name again, Jessica made the other woman stop. Wait. Sure enough, Leslie Ann paused long enough to spot the source of her name. Their eyes met and for a moment, Jessica thought maybe she had the wrong woman since there was something different about the face.

Something off.

"Leslie?" She urged her feet forward through the spring sun-seeking pedestrians to see what was going on.

But without warning, Jess's long-ago roommate sprinted in the opposite direction, shoving through a line at a take-out sandwich restaurant and skidding around a skateboarder.

"Wait!" Jess shouted again, ready to pursue her, but two hands manacled her upper arms from behind.

"Bad, bad idea." Rocco's voice warned in her ear, the low threat in his tone an odd turn-on even as she felt angry about being held back.

Restrained.

"Let go." She stood still, waiting for the fear to kick in, but once again, her body seemed to give Rocco Easton a free pass.

His hands disappeared from her arms, but his body remained so close she could feel the warmth of him through her clothes.

"Do not confront her, Jess." Lightly, he cupped her elbow and turned her to face him. "If you talk to her, you'll be making it very clear that you're on to her and she'll bail out of this town faster than the cops will ever be able to trace."

Jessica still found it difficult to believe someone who'd once been close to her would commit such a personal crime against her. Then again, how many people could have impersonated her so easily? She and Leslie Ann used to enjoy flirting with guys at college parties using each other's names. They never took the game very far since Leslie Ann wasn't into guys any more than Jessica had been at that stage of her life—still walking wounded from the date rape. But it had been fun to impersonate each other's mannerisms. Jessica had even worn a blond wig once when they'd dressed up on Halloween as twins.

Could Leslie Ann have taken the game farther? Far enough to purposely hurt an old friend?

"But I'm not *on* to her. I don't even understand what she's doing or how she's doing it."

She realized she must have raised her voice since a couple of the people waiting in line at the sandwich shop cast curious glances in her direction.

"I can't tell you everything, but I'll bet I can put together a damn accurate picture of what she's been doing if you'll do me a favor and just walk with me back to the truck."

A few people in the sandwich shop line were pointing at her now while others turned to look.

"They think I'm her." Unsettled, she reached for Rocco's arm, eager to get away from the crowd who thought she'd shoved them aside mere moments ago and had miraculously been resurrected at the other end of the street.

"Come on." Rocco hurried her around the corner and back to his truck.

She leaned shamelessly into him, absorbing his strength. Only when she was safely inside the truck did she remember what had seemed off about Leslie Ann's face. Leslie had amazing green eyes, but today when she'd stared at Jessica, her gaze had been dark brown.

The same color as Jessica's.

Sweet Jesus. What if Rocco was right? What if her former best friend was scamming her big-time? Jessica thought about going straight to the police. Yet in her experience, cops were about as easy to deal with as repo men. Well, the repo men of her past. Growing up poor and on the fringes of society had often made cops the enemy, like when they'd chased her out of the good playgrounds for "loitering" since she'd never had parents with her. Or, even more humiliating, when she'd been chased out of the occasional Dumpster because her parents hadn't bought groceries in weeks.

No, she wouldn't go to the cops yet. Her friendship with Leslie Ann warranted the benefit of the doubt, at least until Jessica had time to think it all through.

"I'll be right back." Rocco laid his hand on her shoulder through the passenger-side window. "Don't go anywhere and when I come back we'll start figuring this thing out, okay?"

She nodded absently, not sure how much satisfaction she'd take out of understanding why an old friend wanted to screw her over. Still, as she watched Rocco steal through the small side yard to the garage where they'd seen the Escalade parked, she knew she could find plenty of satisfaction with him another way.

Part of the reason she felt so drained and off her game today was because she hadn't been able to close the deal with Rocco earlier. She'd freaked at being held down and he'd been ready to walk away from her for good. When he'd held her again—both in the truck and on the street—she'd responded to the touches instantly.

Heatedly.

On a day when nothing else made sense in her life, she understood one message loud and clear. She'd found the man who could chase away her sexual ghosts and make her feel like a desirable, whole woman again.

No matter that he was a recovery agent who could re-possess the rug out from under a struggling family, the man she wanted was Rocco Easton.

"WILL YOU TAKE ME home?"

Of all the questions Rocco might have expected when he returned to the truck, he hadn't counted on that one. She seemed so surprised about her so-called friend's betrayal that he figured she'd grill him about the Escalade to search for holes in his identity-theft theory.

Instead, she just wanted to bail.

"You mean your place or the hotel?" He started the engine and waited for direction. He'd need to make a trip back to his place to retrieve his tow truck and his paper-work on the Escalade before he could repossess the vehicle anyway.

"We can go to my apartment…or yours." She slanted a look his way that could mean only one thing.

"You can't be serious." He took his hands off the steering wheel since he had no intention of going anywhere with this woman until she quit giving him the runaround.

"Why?" She straightened, looking for all the world like he'd just offended her.

Rocco surveyed the street, which was quiet except for an occasional dog walker or some kids.

"What do you mean *why?*" He scraped a hand through his hair, frustration simmering even as his mind started spinning visions of him tangled up in bed with her. Settling between her thighs for the night. "Don't you remember what happened earlier today when you thought you wanted more from me?"

At least she had the good grace to blush over that one. She'd left him high and dry without ever giving him any kind of reason. Which—obviously—was anyone's right. But hell, she was crazy if she thought he'd take a second sexual sucker punch in one day.

"I remember."

Her voice was soft and full of emotions he couldn't quite identify, making him realize he'd been harsher than he'd intended.

"That didn't come out right." He couldn't remember the last time he'd needed to apologize to a woman and the words sounded rusty and awkward. "I don't blame you for anything that happened—or didn't happen—earlier. But I was surprised when you stopped and—"

"I was too." Her words were more firm now, her blush replaced with a look of steely determination and a lifted chin. "I was date-raped at seventeen and sometimes the old ghosts of that night still come out to haunt me at the most inopportune moments."

His train of thought went speeding off the tracks as he tried to process that. While her words penetrated his brain, she barreled ahead, not waiting for him to understand.

"Honestly, my stopping didn't have anything to do with

you or what I wanted at the moment. It was more like a temporary freak-out when you were on top of me and I—"

"Christ, I'm so sorry." He reached across the space between the bucket seats and pulled her into his arms, feeling all of two inches tall. "I'm an ass and I'm so sorry you were hurt."

His father had raised him to be more protective of women than this. Rocco's mother had died suddenly of pancreatic cancer when he was six years old and Rocco's upbringing had been shaped by that loss and the need to protect people. He knew you couldn't always see the enemy coming.

But damn it, he should have seen this coming. Thinking back on his encounter with Jess, he could remember exactly when the mood had shifted. When—it seemed so easy to spot now—she panicked.

"It's not your fault." Her words were muffled against his shirt and he loosened his hold a little, unwilling to scare her off or make her uncomfortable.

"I would have understood if you told me." He broke away to hold her at arm's length, probing her eyes for any other secrets she might be withholding.

"I had hoped I'd reached a point in my life where I didn't need to use that as an excuse not to…get close to people."

She wanted sex to be normal again. Now that he knew what was going on, it was so damn easy to read between the lines.

"And that's why you teach the classes." It all made sense. "You wanted to *feel* better in bed, not *be* better in bed."

"Exactly." She grinned unexpectedly and seemed ready to shove the whole conversation aside even though he had about fifty more questions he wanted to ask.

One of which he couldn't suppress.

"Did they catch the guy?" He held himself very still waiting for the answer, his only movement a slow slide of his thumb over her upper arm.

When she hesitated, he had the feeling he wasn't going to like the answer.

"Apparently he skipped town after what happened with me and his address didn't coincide with where he told me he lived." She shrugged. "The police only had my description and a bunch of lies he'd told me to go on."

"Your parents must have been ready to tear the guy's head off." Rocco sure as hell wanted to.

Her crooked smile and shuttered expression told him otherwise.

"That's another story. What do you say we just get out of here and…maybe give me a chance to stick around for the grand finale I missed this morning?"

She still wanted to be with him. That blew his mind, considering he hadn't exactly been Mr. Sensitive before. Something shifted inside Rocco, his every protective instinct coming to the fore.

"Are you sure?" Already the idea of getting her alone again revved his motor faster than the truck's idling engine, even if it meant he'd have to send someone else to retrieve the Escalade.

He'd stuffed down his desire for her only half successfully earlier. There would be no going back if he let himself think about having her now.

"Positively sure."

Her gaze held his, communicated the truth of the statement. But was she plotting her way into his bed because she really wanted him that badly or because she wasn't ready to face the reality of a friend's betrayal?

The humbling thought didn't lessen his desire to fulfill her every wish just the same. She'd clawed her way through some devastating shit. He would do everything in his power to be whatever this woman needed tonight.

"I'd have to call someone to pick up the Escalade. Do you mind if we go to my place instead so I can open the garage and give my guy access to a tow truck?" He forced himself to take deep breaths and make rational plans, determined not to jump all over her at this new green light.

Now that he understood what Jessica had been through, he'd make damn sure their time together eclipsed her past as much as possible. He would work with Jessica's fears to give her as much pleasure as possible. And afterward, maybe she'd trust him enough to help her unravel the mess this Leslie Ann chick was trying to make of her life.

Pleasure and protection. This was one mission he didn't need to be a SEAL to fulfill.

SCOTT WOULD KILL her for this.

Leslie Baylock hid in a ladies' room stall inside a vegan diner two blocks down from her house. Her old house, since she'd have to give it up now that Jessica had found her.

Crying into a piece of single-ply bathroom tissue from the stingy dispenser beside the toilet, Leslie had no idea what to do next. She hadn't succeeded in pulling off a big sting for cash using Jessica's identity. Nor had she successfully brought Jessica into the family fold the way Scott wanted. Those had been her only two objectives as Scott's most trusted first wife, a position of some weight back in the little Colorado town where they lived. A town where he was a well-respected member of the community because of his young and growing family that included three wives and four children, even if Leslie Ann hadn't managed to give him a baby yet.

If she went home without any cash or Jessica, losing her standing among the sister-wives would be the least of her worries, because Scott would beat her as an example to the others. He wasn't supposed to do that. It went against the scriptures of their religion. But Scott didn't care about religion. He cared about control. Authority. Just like she always had.

Damn it.

Blowing her nose on the scrap of tissue, she threw the damp paper in the toilet and flushed. Failure wasn't an option. Leslie had nearly as much control and authority over their extended family—and in their hidden community—as Scott did. They were role models for making polygamy work. All the men in their town envied Scott for his wives, all of whom Leslie had procured personally. And Leslie herself was coveted by every man in town for her skill in selling the lifestyle to the females in her husband's small harem.

She took a lot of pride in that, and she wasn't about to fail now when she finally had the life she wanted. Banging out of the bathroom stall, she washed her face in the sink, rinsing the sweat of fear from her forehead. Leslie had battled her husband's desire for Jessica Winslow before. Scott had wanted Jess desperately when he and Leslie first married in secret. He had drooled over her hot next-door neighbor so badly he'd ended up sneaking behind Leslie's back to ask her out.

Leslie still fought off jealousy that her husband would have sex with a woman unauthorized by *her*. The first wife. The woman who was supposed to have power.

Fury she'd so often suppressed sprang up inside her, propelling her fist forward until she smashed her reflection in the bathroom mirror. She looked just like Jessica. Her friend. Her enemy.

The tweaks to her appearance were necessary to leverage Jessica's credit, but Leslie resented looking like the woman who represented everything Scott wanted—everything Leslie wasn't.

Five years after Scott had taken Jessica, he still couldn't forget her. So Leslie had agreed to bring her into the family as an underling, the lowest ranking wife.

God, the idea hurt more than the spiderweb of cuts snaking across the backs of her knuckles. Blood dripped on the damp tile floor and she couldn't make herself care. She only hoped that, as the lowest ranking spouse, Jessica and the sensual hold she had over Scott could be monitored by the collective wives. Leslie wobbled on her feet from the blood loss, knowing she'd need to stanch the flow soon. But for now, the blood dripping out of her felt like a release, a safety valve on the pressure cooker her life had become. Just a few cuts to relieve stress, nothing a first wife couldn't handle.

All she had to do was make one last economically devastating hit to Jessica's credit to help fund the Baylock family for another year. Then she would kidnap Jessica and help Scott persuade her into marriage.

Jessica would disappear from the San Diego life she knew, a life that was a far cry from her humble beginnings.

But first Leslie would exact a small revenge to help

carry her through the mental torment of sharing her husband with Jessica. Leslie would seduce Jessica's man the same way Jessica had tempted Scott.

And wouldn't that be a fun bit of private revenge that Scott didn't have to know a damn thing about?

FORTY MINUTES LATER, Jessica and Rocco pulled up to a locked gate with no house in sight. Night was falling fast, the sky lit with a last few streaks of purple and red.

They'd driven to Dulzura, a small town south of San Diego and close to the Mexican border. Houses were farther apart here, with expanses of scrub brush and desert valley next to small housing developments and the occasional ranch. She'd been tense with wanting him the whole way here, her body more aware every second this final consummation was delayed.

Damn it, she'd gotten nervous on the way.

"You live here?" She strained her eyes to see ahead.

Rocco lowered the driver's-side window to key in a code on an electric box near the gate.

"Home sweet home."

"On first impression, it seems more like Fort Knox." The gate security and the big spread only added to her nerves. How rich was this guy? "How far away is the house?"

"Right there." He pointed out a sprawling ranch home as they rounded a turn and climbed a small hill.

The Spanish-influenced stucco and red-tile structure boasted multiple rooflines and fat columns along a front veranda.

"Nice." It was a total understatement, but she couldn't help a twinge of feeling out of her league. The apartments she'd lived in growing up had been the size of his double garage.

She was trusting him with so much and she couldn't help second-guessing herself given the way one of her few close friends had apparently betrayed her.

"Well, it's not exactly draped in velvet and swimming in candelabras like one of your workshop settings, but it works for me." He pulled up to the garage without opening it and shut off the truck.

It struck Jessica that he must think the place looked sparse through her eyes, when in fact she'd been more than a little intimidated to see the size of his private spread. Opting to let him keep that illusion until she got her bearings on foreign terrain, she unfastened her seat belt.

"According to my workshop on Seduced by Surroundings, any place can be a sensual haven with a little effort."

While Rocco came around to open her door, she wondered how much conversational mileage she could leverage from her lecture notes to cover her edginess.

"You might revise that opinion once you come inside." He held out his hand to help her down and she took it, surprised that such a discreet amount of contact could generate an electric jolt even with her bout of nerves.

Then again, her attraction to him had started when she laid her hands on him for the erotic massage lesson. One touch and she was hooked. Her heart rate jumped up its pace.

"Why? Did you decorate with posters of your favorite rock icons and babes bending over the hood of a car?" She needed to keep talking to take her mind off the fact that she had actively pursued a man and now planned to sleep with him.

She was so keyed up she feared another bout of performance anxiety despite the endorphins his touch had generated. If only she could delay things just a little until she found her nerve for seduction again.

"I don't know that there was any decorating involved, actually. I more or less just bought whatever seemed fun to me." He disarmed an alarm system beside the front door while she took in the red tile floor in the arched courtyard.

"Well, I think I'm ready for fun today considering my identity is probably being abused by a woman I considered a friend. And the most important workshop I've ever given didn't receive my full attention because I'm scared I'll wake up Monday morning and find out my credit cards are no good or my worldly possessions are going to be carted away by an army of recovery agents." Jessica couldn't quit babbling, her mouth as overcome with anxiety as the rest of her.

She stopped short inside the foyer, the acoustics of the round room making her voice bounce back to her.

Rocco flipped a light switch and a cast-iron chandelier brightened overhead. She had a vague impression of a sunken living area to one side, but he pointed her past it toward the back of the house where more archways repeated the pattern she'd just seen outside. The walls were painted with dark colors and the doors were made of heavy woods, but the effect would be cool and soothing during the hot months. Ceramic tile flowed from one room to the next, connecting the house in brick-colored stone.

"Come on." He took her hand again, his gentle touch both more exciting and more familiar each time she felt it.

Part of her wanted to pull away as he seemed to haul her

toward the bedroom with no prelude. But then, she'd propositioned him. This was what she wanted, right?

Nervous flutters centered in her belly, but when he tugged her into the room at the end of the corridor, she didn't see a bed or a nightstand or anything else that belonged in a guy's bedroom. He'd brought her into a study or a den, she guessed, although there were no books or desks either. Just polished hardwood floors and a few photos of him in uniform scattered on the walls, his arm slung around smiling foreigners. The photos made her smile, but what took her eye even more firmly was the fact that she was now surrounded by arcade-style video games.

Damn it, how would she ever overcome her fears if she didn't just dive into the main act already? But even as part of her screamed in frustration, she couldn't help but smile at this brief reprieve. Maybe he'd sensed her nervousness.

"You see? No decorating involved. I just crammed them all in here." He approached the Frogger machine and pressed play. "I even rigged it so I don't have to use quarters."

Jessica walked deeper into the room, surprised by this new facet of the Navy SEAL turned repo man. He did have a less intense side. A playful side, even.

He was also damn insightful, giving her a few minutes to get her scattered emotions together before they launched into the main event. Gratitude mingled with a surge of renewed desire.

"You've got Pac-Man." She only played a few times as a kid when she'd found spare change around the payphones in a pizza joint near one of the crappy buildings she'd lived in during junior high.

"Want to try your luck while I get us something to eat?"

She took a deep breath, relaxed into this slower pace of his and decided to go with the flow. Maybe delaying gratification would make the pay off all the more delectable.

"Sure, but I'll warn you." She was already pressing the start button. The glow of neon light filled the screen and a happy tune sang out of the box. "You might not be able to pry me away."

"It just so happens I enjoy a challenge." He turned for the door and not even the flashing head on the video screen could keep her eyes from checking out his butt in khakis.

Rocco embodied the promise of great sex and unlimited fun, and Jessica knew it would be all too easy to lose focus on her business needs and the identity crisis looming over her head. But surely this one brief time out from real life couldn't make things any worse.

As she maneuvered the munching mouth around the screen, she ignored the twitch in her neck that told her otherwise.

8

Two hours later, with both of them fed and the dishes cleaned, Rocco cheered Jessica's attempt to beat her own record. She'd already surpassed his high score and that of two other contenders to take a place in the top ten. He enjoyed watching her. He'd only stepped away briefly to call his father and make sure he'd taken his medicine. Then he'd contacted his friend Laz to ask if he could solicit a hand from his uncle on the SDPD to help Jess. But other than that, Rocco had spent every possible second studying the woman obsessed with Pac-Man.

He knew part of her video game craze came from an attack of nerves about being here. About sleeping with him when she still battled private demons where sex was concerned.

He understood that, and that was why he'd shown her the game room. His collection of twenty-seven machines had provided entertainment for everyone who'd ever come to his house, which—sadly—had been only his SEAL friends up until now.

But watching Jessica play was a thrill all its own. He'd been turned-on for the past two hours, but the delay in the big event would be worth it because she was relaxed. Comfortable. That could only bode well for when he got her in the bedroom.

As he sat in a swiveling captain's chair near the television in a corner of the room, he wondered how Jessica had snuck under his radar so easily when he'd kept women at arm's length for most of his life.

Her lips pursed in concentration and her hair slid strand by strand over her shoulder as she leaned forward. She swept the red mass behind her back approximately every six minutes. Yes, he'd kept track. Her body swayed in time with her hands on the controls, her shoulders steering the way she wanted her character to go and her hips following a second later. She'd ditched the jacket that went with the pinstripe navy suit, her skirt cupping the shape of her curves without anything to obstruct the view.

He'd mentally undressed her at least fifty times since he'd sat down. Rocco told himself that was just solid tactical strategy—he needed to make tonight just right for her. But his head warred with totally selfish desires versus what he thought would make her lose all inhibition and give herself over to the heat that awaited them.

"Damn." She bit her lip, her face lit by the glow of neon lights from the screen. Her hands worked harder to coax the end result she sought.

He suspected that trait had dominated her life the way it had his. When the world didn't offer up the rewards they wanted, they simply worked harder to obtain them. He'd never minded that approach for himself, but it rankled to think she'd had to live that way.

Her game came to an end and she hopped around in a

victory dance in bare feet, her high heels gone the way of her jacket. In some of his fantasies, she then walked over to him and made the first move, her long legs bracketing his hips as she straddled his lap.

"I'm in eighth place," she crowed, turning to look at him with one fist pumping the air while the video game sang a victory tune.

Her hand stilled above her head as their eyes met. Held.

Perhaps some of his intentions were broadcast in his expression, because her mouth opened on a round note but no sound came out.

Her hand fell to her side.

"Have you had enough time to play?" He didn't want to rush her, so he thought it just as well he stayed in his seat.

Fingers gripping the arms of the chair, Rocco held himself back, swallowing the urge to trace the seams of her skirt with his hands.

"Depends. What other games do you have in mind?" She tilted her head to one side and seemed to size him up, the move one-hundred-percent seductress.

He flexed his hands on the armrests, so freaking tempted.

"No games." For his sanity. And for her comfort until she trusted him completely. "I want you way too much right now."

"Would it be different between us tonight if you weren't…trying to be careful with me?"

The question spoke of an innocence he hadn't fully appreciated up until now. The idea that she'd developed a whole business plan around sensuality when she had relatively little experience with full-blown sex did more than intrigue him. It stirred hot, primal urges to educate her.

"Yes." He ground out the answer, his voice more thick with hunger than eloquent.

"How?" She took a step closer but didn't touch him. "I'd like to know what I'm missing."

He debated. Worked the wisdom of her request over in his head. Spinning out the details for her might be a slow form of torture for him. But he guessed her curiosity was a sign of desire and he gambled that answering her questions had the potential to stir a deeper longing.

"I would have never let you amuse yourself for so long without me." He glanced in the direction of the game she'd been trying to beat. "And I would have come up behind you to help you play."

"You think you have better moves than me?" She grinned, teasing him. But her entry-level flirtation was no match for the thoughts he was having about her.

His eyes roamed up her legs, slowing at her thighs and burning over her breasts before arriving at her face.

"I would have pulled aside your hair to kiss the back of your neck." He'd dreamed up so many ways he could have approached her, and that was his personal favorite. "I would have pinned your hips against the machine with mine until you didn't care about the game anymore."

"You think the feel of you would have made me quit the game?" She wrapped her arms around herself as if to ward off a chill.

Or a shiver.

"I wouldn't mind if you kept playing. But it wouldn't have stopped me from sliding down the zipper on the side of your skirt."

He didn't need to look away from her face to know she felt for the teeth of the metal fastening with her fingers.

"You're very observant." Her hand remained on her hip. "It's mostly covered by the blouse."

"I can see through your top when the bright screens flash on the video game." Something about the blue light penetrated the thin white cotton and, while it didn't make the blouse see-through, it certainly gave him more to think about. To lust over.

She reached for the buttons on the front of the shirt, her hands steady as she unfastened the first one.

"If you already know what's in store for you, I can't see any need to leave it on, can you?" She reached for the second button and then the third before he found his voice.

"No." He'd be ripping the armrests right off the damn chair at this rate. "Leave it on. That is—I hope you'll let me undress you."

The air seemed thick and hot, as if the AC had kicked off to let the Southern California heat have its way with them.

"And if you had your way you'd go with the skirt first?" She took another step toward him and this time her bare knee brushed his khaki-clad leg.

Memories from her belly dancing class returned. This woman was no stranger to using her body for seductive purposes, even if she hadn't put the knowledge into practice very often. Had this touch been carefully designed? Premeditated to make him go wild?

Their eyes connected and he didn't know who was baiting who anymore. Unable to stop himself, he reached for her zipper and lowered the tab until her skirt slid down her hips to the floor. He would watch her every second for any sign of unease to make sure she was never scared. Only turned-on.

Creamy skin surrounded the tiniest triangle of intricate navy-blue lace. Earlier today she'd had a pink rhinestone-studded cutout of a heart on one hip; now there was a silver belly chain riding low around the waist of her panties.

Even more interesting was the excess length of chain that dangled down to the top of her thigh. Three tiny pearls teased up against her leg, a mere inch or two from the place he'd most like to put his tongue.

"If looks could provide orgasms, I think I would be a very happy woman right now." She shifted from one foot to the other and he realized some of her nervousness had returned.

He needed to distract her, keep her focused on all the amazing sensations waiting right there for her.

Rising to his feet, he stood toe to toe with her long enough to see her breathing speed up and her pulse throb at the base of her throat.

He slid an arm around her waist and walked her backward.

"I'm taking you to my bedroom. Are you okay with that?"

She nodded, her feet stumbling but moving. Her eyes showed no fear, only anticipation.

"Please hurry." Her voice slid along his senses like a silky caress, barely there but sexy as hell.

Steering her around a sofa, he crossed the living room to the master suite. The lights were off in his bedroom, but he could still see her thanks to the spill-over glow from the hallway.

Not waiting to get her to the bed, he traced the path of the chain around her waist with one finger, pulling her to a stop in the middle of the floor.

"I like this." The links fit tight together in a close weave of silver, making a smooth, seamless band against her skin.

"I try to wear things that make me feel sexy even when…I don't necessarily live sexy."

The admission socked him in the gut, stirring anger along with an overriding desire to find the guy who had hurt her. Hell, he might have found all the reason he'd ever need to think seriously about becoming a cop.

He reined in that anger, gentled his touch. His voice.

"Apparently we agree what's hot." He allowed his forefinger and thumb to slide down the excess length of chain that dangled in front of her panties. "That bodes well for tonight."

He stroked over the small pearls at the end of the chain and then pressed them against her mound. Rolling. Rubbing.

Her only answer was a sharp cry of need as her knees seemed to fold. She wrapped her arms around him, giving herself over to him completely.

Yes.

The hum of victory sang in his veins. Jessica had spent years learning how to turn "feeling good" into an art form for her work, but he'd stake his life she felt better than ever right now.

Her breasts flattened against him, the scent of sweet feminine flesh filling his nostrils. He worked the pearls down the front of her panties and bent his head to taste the swell of creamy skin above the line of her bra.

She tunneled her fingers through his hair and a ragged moan escaped her lips. Plying the pearls gently along the inside of her thigh, he lifted the edge of her panties and then slipped them inside the lace.

"Roc—" She cut short his name as he rolled the small ornament across the swollen bud between her legs.

He swallowed back the memories that abbreviated name implied. The Rock. Thank God he could lose himself in her instead of falling under the weight of who he'd been a lifetime ago. He pulled down the cup of her bra to expose a pebble-hard nipple and stroked the tight point with his tongue.

"Rocco, wait." She straightened, taking her breasts with her as she arched back to make eye contact. "I can't—I don't want—no orgasms for me until after you. I don't want any time to think. I just want to feel."

He could have argued that he would give her multiple Os without any great effort, but he knew that it was important for her to call the shots this time.

"Anything." He just wanted a bed. A condom.

He walked her backward, releasing the pearls on her belly chain to tug down her panties. Her hands reached for her shirt and she unfastened the last few buttons, her fingers flying to dispense with the shirt.

Until the backs of her legs hit the bed.

Her eyes widened. Nervous? He couldn't tell for sure.

"Tell me what you want." He finished peeling her shirt off, then made quick work of the front clasp of her bra. "Don't spare a detail."

She blinked. Her tongue slid across her lips to moisten her mouth.

"Me on top." Shrugging off the straps of her bra, she stood naked except for the panties and the silver chain at her waist.

Hooking a finger in the waist of her underwear, he tugged them down her legs until gravity took over and they slid to the floor.

"I can think of ten different ways to have you on top of me, all without even getting creative." He molded her breasts to fit his hands, the soft flesh spilling out of his palm as he rolled one nipple and then the other between his fingers.

"Nothing creative necessary. I want you in me." She palmed his erection to back up the words and he damn near swayed on his feet.

Jessica hoped she was going to get sex right this time. She felt so good. So, so good.

She couldn't stand for anything else to go wrong or any stupid thoughts to screw with her head. Only Rocco could screw with her.

The idea made her breathless.

She tugged down his zipper and slid her hand inside his boxers to feel him skin on skin. The heat of him kindled an answering swirl of arousal between her hips.

"I've been waiting for this for so long." She knew she probably shouldn't have let that slip, but the words were more for her, a wishful utterance to cap off a long bedroom dry spell.

Rocco shoved off his khakis and his boxers. He must have stepped out of his shoes earlier. The sight of so much naked muscle and man...

She liked it.

Her whole body trembled as if it was her first time, and, damn it, she wished it was. This was the way sex should be. Hot. Deliberate.

He shaped her breasts in his strong hands and she melted. Her hips tilted toward his, hungry for the hard feel of him. His hips pushed back and she opened to him, lifting her leg to wrap around his thigh.

With a chest-rattling growl he spun them so that he fell on the bed first, drawing her down on top of him. She couldn't breathe. Couldn't think.

No workshop on pleasure could have prepared her for what Rocco made her feel. The ripple of muscle in the thighs between her open legs sent a shiver of longing through her whole body.

She wanted to be possessed by him.

The truth of that simple human need wrapped around her with more happiness than she'd ever imagined sex could bring. She wasn't just aroused beyond belief.

She was healed.

"Please," Jessica whispered to him, unable to keep the desperation out of her voice. "Oh, please."

Sitting up, she positioned her sex over his shaft and slid along the veined ridge. He was thick and hard. Hot and incredibly heavy.

Exquisite.

He reached for a prophylactic from the nightstand, his hand patting around a drawer while she brought herself close to the ultimate pleasure simply by rubbing against him.

He lifted her up to sheathe himself in one effortless move. She scarcely got to enjoy the feel of his hands on her hips before he was lowering her. Positioning the tip of his cock right where she needed him most.

She held still for a moment, wanting to savor the lush sensations of it all, but she was drowning in them. Rocco placed his thumbs on either side of her sex and rubbed the sensitive flesh as he edged his way inside her.

Jessica lost all focus as she opened herself to him. To pleasure.

His thumbs found a rhythm that sent her hurtling through the stars and her whole body convulsed. Any control she had was relinquished in that moment. She shuddered, fingers twisting in the blanket behind him until he sat up. He moved to the edge of the bed, keeping her on his lap. On the strong seat of his thighs.

Sagging in his arms, she gave herself over to his demands, her body gladly giving him everything. She kissed his shoulder, his neck. Tasted the light sheen of sweat on his skin.

Fingers playing over her nipple, he slowed the pace while she caught her breath. She barely had enough energy left to cry out his name when he sent her flying off that sexual ledge all over again, her womb contracting sharply with his every toe-curling thrust.

He let himself follow her this time, his muscles rigid as he stroked his way through the last of her aftershocks.

The moment was as sweetly beautiful as anything her wistful imagination had ever envisioned. Being held in Rocco's arms and feeling so completely connected to him rendered her speechless. Overwhelmed.

She was so caught off guard by the immensity of it that she felt very grateful for the dark of the room and the utter quiet as they lay together afterward. Rocco pulled a blanket up from the foot of the bed to cover her, but neither seemed to feel any great need to speak or to sort out the convoluted turns of their relationship.

All her adult life Jessica had wanted to find someone who could make sex feel more than just safe—she'd wanted someone who could make it thrilling and erotic too. Now that she'd had that experience, she knew she'd never be satisfied with a relationship built on that one component. Some people were totally content to have no-strings affairs or one-night stands, but she wasn't that type of person. Her sexual well-being was too hard won to risk it with multiple partners.

And underneath the physical attraction, what did she and Rocco share?

His work ripped things out of the hands of people who really needed a break in life. Having had most of her own small treasures yanked away as a child, she couldn't come to terms with Rocco's job.

Peering over at him in the light filtering in from the living room, she thought for the first time about the people he worked for instead of the people he visited with his repo truck. Now that her credit was under attack with this identity-theft issue, she could see what it felt like to have your good intentions taken out from under you.

Was that how it felt for Rocco's father, who owned the Escalade someone hadn't bothered to pay for? She supposed the vehicle could injure his business credit. And multiple vehicles that weren't paid for could easily cripple his business.

The realization made her a little less comfortable with her old notions about recovery agents. Still, there were honest people who simply needed a break to get their feet under them, and the repo system hurt them. She wondered if Rocco ever felt that way about his work or if he only saw the other side.

He'd treated her so tenderly tonight that it was tough to believe he'd embraced a career that seemed callous in her book.

Yet, callous or not, he'd shown her something magical tonight. He'd returned to her a piece of herself that had been missing for a very long time. And no matter how fast they parted company next week, she'd owe this sexy ex-SEAL a very big debt.

9

SEEING JESSICA OUT in the barn among his horses the next day made Rocco nervous.

Not that he was afraid for her safety—his horses were too well mannered to kick or bite. No, he felt nervous because she looked so damn at home in one of his T-shirts, which was large enough to almost cover her skirt from the day before. With her hair up in a messy knot and her scrubbed-clean skin, she had the appearance of a woman who belonged here. In his house. In his life.

Just the thought gave him hives. He'd never brought another woman out here. Ever. This was his space, his he-man lair, where he kept his four-wheeler and his dirt bike, his horses and a convertible Mustang he'd rebuilt with his dad as a teen. He'd retreated here when he came home from overseas, burned by a treacherous woman and his own body.

Now, instead of Jessica begging to get the hell out of his haven, the sensuality maven had the nerve to look totally at home in a horse stall—and she nursed a love of Pac-Man.

"Morning." He figured he'd stick with the basics until he got a feel for any changes in the wind.

While he may not have brought any women out to his home, he'd certainly logged enough intimate encounters to know that sex changed everything and a guy would have to be brainless not to see it. The one time he'd let his guard down on a morning after, he'd wound up walking home through a land-mine field and losing key mobility in his leg for maintaining his SEAL status.

Of course, he had been fortunate enough to discover his bed partner was playing both sides of a dangerous spy game before he compromised anything sensitive. But it had pissed him off after he'd been so damn careful, only sleeping with her after he'd been introduced to her by military-higher ups. Too bad she'd had more people than him fooled....

"Hi." Jessica grinned, patting his horse's nose and looking about as far removed from a leggy double agent as was possible. "What's this guy's name?"

She pointed to the white-and-gray yearling he'd purchased recently.

"Nobody's Business. His name was half the reason I bought him." He could talk horses all day. It was the relationship thing that proved tough. "I got a call well after midnight last night. The Escalade was already gone by the time my guys got to Chula Vista to pick it up. I put a call in to the cops to check out your friend's address, but my guess is she's long gone after she saw you yesterday."

Her hand paused on the horse's nose.

"If I wasn't responsible for the missing vehicle in the first place, I sure feel like I'm responsible now." She chewed her lip. "I scared her off because I wanted to speak to her."

"She's the one who's up to no good, Jess. Not you."

Dipping a bucket into the bag of oats, he passed it to her to feed the Thoroughbred too slow to make it as a racehorse but fast enough to be one of Rocco's personal favorites.

"I'm sorry I didn't listen to you. I should have stayed in the truck." She shook her head. "About last night—"

Here we go.

"I don't regret a second of it, but I do think I'd better get home and—" She shrugged as she dumped the oats into the bucket inside the animal's stall. "I appreciate you making me aware that Leslie Ann seems to be impersonating me. So if you felt like you owed me anything before, you've certainly paid me back with interest by bringing the identity theft to light."

"What do you mean *seems to be* impersonating you?" He tried not to be offended that Jessica was cutting and running before he could. That should be good, right?

Except he was incensed. Indignant.

"You have no idea how close we were as teenagers when I moved into my first foster home. Leslie was supportive. Accepting. She even doled out clothes from her closet to help keep me from being labeled a charity case."

"You were in a foster home?" He set aside his other concerns for the moment to pick up this fact he'd somehow missed.

"My parents rarely bothered to send me to school and eventually I had a guidance counselor who got mad enough about it that she got the foster-care system involved." She shrugged as if that chapter of her life didn't mean much to her even though it had to have been a hellish experience. "The foster home was an improvement, of sorts. Living next to Leslie Ann was one of the high points of my time with the family who took me in. She was really good to me."

"People change." Damn it, he knew that firsthand.

People could surprise the ever-loving hell out of you—right before they stabbed you in the back.

But maybe Jessica was more concerned with protecting herself from getting close to him than she was with making sure Leslie Ann was punished for her actions.

Wasn't that a humbling thought?

"I realize that. And I know it looks like Leslie Ann is the guilty party, especially now that she's disappeared again, but I can't figure out why she would turn from being a friend to trying to hurt me this much. It doesn't make sense."

"Whether it makes sense or not, you need to take action before this chick ruins every dollar's worth of credit you ever possessed." He kicked at the straw on the floor, spreading it out to cover a bare patch where wooden floorboards showed through.

He wanted to protect her, but he was afraid if he pushed the issue too hard she'd only put more distance between them.

"I've already called the credit card companies and I've contacted the police. We *both* have. I'm glad that you alerted me to a bigger problem and I will definitely take every measure necessary to stop it from happening again."

Straightening, she stepped away from the horse and Nobody's Business looked at her with big, sad eyes.

Jesus, had she won over all his animals too?

"But?" He could hear it haunting her words even if she didn't say it.

"But I'd better return to my house this morning if you don't mind taking me. Or I can just call a cab."

"A cab?" Anger simmered. He might be ready to nip any romantic thoughts in the bud, but he didn't send women home alone in cabs. "Not a chance. I'll give you a ride wherever you want to go."

A moment passed before she nodded.

"Thanks. I'll just go grab my things."

His horse whinnied for her as she walked out of the stable and Rocco couldn't help but feel just as abandoned.

THE RIDE BACK to the hotel was damn chilly considering she'd spent all night wrapped around the man beside her in the full-size pickup.

They went the first ten minutes without saying much of anything to each other beyond a few comments from her on the weather and a couple of unintelligible grunts from him. Now, as they closed the distance to Coronado Island, she figured she'd better step up her conversational efforts if she wanted to salvage any kind of friendship with Rocco. Although she'd hoped to ease back on the intimacy between them, she hadn't intended to sever communication completely.

"I'm sorry if I came across kind of…abrupt this morning." She didn't know how else to put it.

He drummed the steering wheel softly, as if he could conjure up the right words.

"I knew, going into last night, that it wasn't going to be simple."

Jessica considered that response. It hadn't been quite what she'd expected. She stared out the windshield to avoid looking at him and being tempted all over again. He'd put to rest her reservations about sex. If only she could relax about relationships as well, but she sensed a big wall between them and suspected he'd added as many bricks to that barrier as she had. There was a remoteness about him that would be tough for any woman to break through, let alone someone like her who was steeped in issues all her own.

"You like your sexual encounters to be simple?"

"Time out." He shook his head as he maneuvered the truck through a patch of Sunday-morning traffic and a throng of pedestrians crossing the street in their church clothes. "Let's not assume the worst of each other, okay?"

"Right." She nodded, acknowledging the value of such a simple piece of wisdom. If her parents had only thought to draw up some ground rules for arguments, her childhood might not have been half-bad.

Growing up poor would have been so much easier if her mom and dad had been remotely functional as parents. She'd forgiven them long ago, but life still had the power to surprise her with all the ways she'd missed out and messed up because she didn't know any better when it came to relationships.

Rocco accelerated once the street cleared again. "I'm just saying that I should have been a little more—I don't know—tuned in this morning when you wanted to head home. From what you told me about your past experience, I should have realized you wouldn't exactly be ready to spend the day on the four-wheeler with me."

She grinned. "After last night, I think the four-wheeler would be pushing your luck either way."

The pleasurable soreness in her body had taken her by surprise this morning. She would have been content to simply stay in bed with Rocco all day long, but she knew the longer they were with each other, the more awkward the parting would become.

They rolled to a stop at a streetlight, which made it all too easy for him to look her right in the eyes again.

"You told me that the cops could never find the guy who…hurt you." He stared at her across the truck cab. "Did *you* ever look for him?"

"No." Her chest got tight remembering what he'd gotten away with. Scott Baylock had disappeared as if he'd never existed. "That is, I was terrified to see him for the next year and a half, and I spent a lot of time scanning the faces in every crowd to make sure I spotted him before he found me if he was still in town. But I never did see him again."

She'd been so grateful to win a scholarship to a school in the Midwest. The academic opportunity had lifted her out of her dysfunctional family and offered her a chance to make something of herself. At the same time, it had decreased the possibility of her ever running into Scott again and she'd thrived in the small community. Leslie Ann— her neighbor her last two years in the foster home—had followed her to the school. They'd had fun rooming together until Leslie Ann got homesick and had returned to Colorado.

"Did the cops just give up?" Rocco's disgust at the thought was evident in every word.

"I don't know. I certainly did after I didn't hear anything about an arrest for six months." She shifted in her seat. "Do you think we could not talk about it?"

"Sure thing." He pulled into the hotel parking lot and wound his way through the brunch traffic to where her vehicle was parked. "It looks like you're going to have bigger worries on your mind anyhow."

Jessica's eyes locked on the scene before her.

A tow truck had her Escalade on the flatbed trailer, and the driver was getting into a cab marked First-Rate Recovery.

"They're repossessing the wrong car." She couldn't believe it. Two repo men in one weekend, and this guy didn't look like he was going to be talked out of his job.

"Hey!" Jessica shouted to him as she leaped from Rocco's truck. "Wait!"

Waving her arms, she tried to get the guy's attention, but he was already shifting into gear. Son of a—

"I'll follow him," Rocco shouted from his truck. "This guy's a crook anyway."

She wondered if he meant that literally or just in the general "all repo men are bad apples" kind of way. Considering Rocco ran the same kind of business, she imagined the former.

As she watched Rocco's pickup chase her Escalade out of the parking lot, it occurred to her that slipping out of her relationship with Rocco wasn't going to be half as easy as she'd expected.

"I'M AFRAID there's not much we can do."

Jessica was better braced for the words this time since she'd heard the same spiel from the desk cop who'd taken her statement earlier that morning. In an attempt to be proactive, she'd insisted on speaking to a higher-up to learn more about her options, but the guy was no more help than his predecessor.

"But she impersonated me." Jessica set down the cardboard cup of surprisingly decent java. Still, good caffeine didn't make up for having a crime totally written off. "Doesn't that count for something? Isn't impersonating someone to discredit them and steal from them a fairly serious offense?"

"Ms. Winslow, it's like this." The older cop hunkered down on the counter across from her. He'd walked her down to the far end, away from the winos and assorted riffraff that filled the station on a Monday morning. "The problem is so common that we could spend all our time on stuff like this."

"But—"

"It's also a nonviolent crime, which forces us to put it lower on the list, beneath the murdering and raping scum I see come through here every week."

Jessica straightened, unnerved by the cop's frankness. She wondered if Scott Baylock would have gotten away if this guy had been on the case. He looked like he wasn't afraid to mete out a little frontier justice if the situation called for it.

"I see." Nodding, she spun her earring around in her lobe and tried to think what else she could say to change his mind.

She came up blank.

"My advice is that you contact the credit card company and get their insurance guys on the case. That's what they make the big bucks for, you know what I'm saying?" He snapped a piece of gum and grinned.

"Yes. Absolutely. I'll do that." She pounded the wide counter with her fist to release her lingering frustration over getting nowhere today. "Thank you for your help, Officer."

She had no idea if that was the proper title, but he tipped his hat and smiled back at her, no doubt pleased to have shuffled her out of the station.

Damn it.

She stalked back to the Escalade with a copy of the police report in hand, the shining sun mocking her overcast mood. Rocco had returned the SUV to her late last night after he'd confronted one of his repo rival. When he'd pointed out the incorrect VIN, the guy had released her vehicle, but that didn't stop Rocco from being up in arms about the whole thing. His father wasn't supposed to contract with any recovery businesses save his, and he couldn't understand how a rival firm had found out about the Escalade.

Jessica had been too tired to quiz him on the ins and outs of the second repossession, plus she'd been afraid of falling straight into his arms if she stood too close to him for more than a minute. Just because she knew she shouldn't mess around with a man who was only interested in sex for sex's sake didn't mean it was easy to resist him.

Firing up the SUV, Jessica wound through the traffic toward her office. She would be late this morning after her stop at the police station, but the insurance company had demanded the paperwork to show she'd gone that route. Ten minutes later she was parking in front of her offices, a tiny patch of space in a dying strip mall in the northern end of town. She didn't really need much in the way of a storefront and the rent was cheap here.

"Morning." She breezed past her part-time secretary, a sweet retiree who wanted to earn just enough to supplement her Social Security check. Mrs. Teraza worked longer hours during the months when her grandkids had birthdays, but the holiday season was, hands down, her most industrious time of year.

"What are you doing back already?" Mrs. Teraza took

her glasses off her head where they'd been propped by a floppy, folded-over ponytail she wore like a high bun.

"What do you mean?" Jessica slowed, going over the police officer's notes on the crime report. "I've been gone all weekend. You knew I would be in today, right?"

Jess admired her assistant's outfit—a knee-length tweed skirt and white blouse that she rocked with an old-fashioned prep-school sweater in deep burgundy. Mrs. Teraza's legs were still so cute she could have lined right up with the cheerleaders in the homecoming parade and no one would guess she wasn't still seventeen from the knees down.

"You went home to change?" She eyed Jessica like a doctor trying to make a diagnosis on a patient who was too ill to speak for herself.

And just what would make Mrs. Teraza think she'd changed her outfit? The woman did go around the office without her eyeglasses on half the time. She wore them around her neck more often than she put them up to her baby blues and heaven knows, the elderly lady needed the extra lenses to help keep her world in focus.

"I was just at the police station and no I did not change. What makes you think I did?" A shaky sort of fear crawled through her limbs as she began to realize what might have happened.

What couldn't have happened.

"My dear, you were just in here ten minutes ago with a killer little vintage suit that looked liked something I might have worn a few decades ago." She eyed Jessica's outfit— a cream-colored skirt with a gold silk tank—up and down. "Whatever did you do with it?"

Oh God.

"Nothing." Jessica reached for Mrs. Teraza's desk for support as her whole world seemed to tip sideways. "I didn't wear that suit and I wasn't in here earlier. Someone has been impersonating me and she's getting bolder every day."

"I don't believe it." Mrs. Teraza shook her head, her eyes scrunched in surprise. "She did rush the good mornings a bit, but you tend to do that on Mondays anyway. She went straight into the office and—"

"What?" Jessica straightened at the look on the other woman's face. The lines around her eyes smoothed as her complexion turned ghostly pale.

"She asked for the client list." She clutched the lapel of her prep-school sweater.

"You gave her my client information?" Jessica's voice notched up a breathless octave as she tried to understand the implications of why someone—Leslie Ann?—would have any interest in stealing the database she had worked so hard to build.

"I thought I was giving *you* the client information." Mrs. Teraza clutched her arm. "I'm so sorry, sweetie, but I never would have guessed—"

"It's okay." Jessica patted her arm, reassuring herself as much as the older woman. "I've already talked to the cops, but I'll go back again and tell them about this. Maybe I'd better check my office first to see if anything else is missing."

Bumping into the wicker wastebasket on her way, she moved toward the small adjoining room she'd turned into her workspace.

"Why would someone want to pretend to be you?"

Why indeed? She wasn't mega successful yet, with her business just getting off the ground. She'd never had much in the way of money, with every cent she'd ever made going into her company in one way or another.

And her family…she'd given up trying to keep track of their drifter whereabouts a few years after she'd finished college.

"I honestly can't imagine." But she'd gone from annoyed and frustrated to extremely worried.

Having someone impersonate her to buy a car was one thing. Having someone stroll right into her life and pass herself off as Jessica Winslow, that went beyond freaky.

As Jessica searched around her office for signs of anything that might be missing, Mrs. Teraza stirred the pot by suggesting the impersonator could be out for revenge, or that the woman might have an extreme case of jealousy. At one point, she even went so far as to suggest Jessica might have an evil twin she'd never known about.

And then Mrs. Teraza gasped. A long, lung-burning inhalation.

"What?" Jess put down the police report she'd been carrying.

"Maybe she wants to kill you and then take over your life."

She suggested it with such perfect seriousness—the right mixture of fear and disbelief—that Jessica actually weighed the possibility before realizing how preposterous it sounded.

"That's ridiculous."

Still, now she was downright scared. The time had come to help the police track down Leslie Ann and see if—or damn it, *why*—her old roommate was causing all this grief. Either way, Jessica needed more answers and she wouldn't be able to get any work done until she had them.

She found herself reaching for the phone. She couldn't squelch the urge to call Rocco to see if he had any ideas for finding the missing woman. Obviously, in his line of work he'd faced this kind of problem before.

She liked to think that growing up first in a dysfunctional family and then, later, in foster homes had made her strong. That she could conquer her fears on her own. But years of counseling had taught her that she needed to reach out for help sometimes.

Yes, she had to work up the courage to face Leslie Ann James head-on. And if Rocco could help her do that, she needed to call him. Because she could no longer ignore the probability that someone was out to steal her life altogether.

10

Rocco rang Jessica's bell, surprised she wanted to see him after her obvious attempts to keep things light between them that morning.

She hadn't exactly eaten her words in the voice mail message she'd left, but then, she might not recognize the hot-and-cold nature of her behavior. Someone had done such a number on her that she didn't have a lot of relationship experience to draw from.

Fury still tightened his chest when he thought about what had happened to her. And the fact that the guy had never been caught? He just might call Laz this week and tell him to set up the test for the police academy. He'd make finding the scum-sucking bastard his first piece of business once he had a badge.

Then again, what was stopping him from making it a priority even without one?

"Come in," Jessica called from inside the condo apartment.

Her building was a long stretch of two-story townhomes with downstairs patios and upstairs terraces. Her unit was in the middle and he'd double-checked the house number since there were no plants or doormats, no wind chimes or any hint that the sensuality guru lived here.

Opening the door, he found her apartment dark and cool compared to the bright heat of the day outside. And why the hell wasn't she keeping her door locked?

"I can't even see." He squinted through a small foyer into what he guessed must be the main living area, but she had blinds drawn all over the place.

"It keeps it cool." Her voice sounded low and throaty. Like she had a cold?

Or like she was thinking about sex?

The possibility had his feet moving toward the sound.

"Are you feeling hot?" He could make out some low sectional furniture and modern-looking black shelves filled with books and—here and there—lit candles.

"Not as hot as you're going to be in about five minutes." Her voice was closer, just to one side of him.

He turned to see her, but a swath of silk fell over his face and covered his eyes.

His heart rate doubled, pounding with the force of his want for her.

"Just what did you have in mind?" He felt around the silk sash at his eyes, sensing her behind him.

She drew the ends of the cloth tight and tied them into a knot at the back of his head. He wanted to reach around and grab her, plant her against the wall and have his way with her, but no sooner had she tied his blindfold than she danced out of reach.

"I thought we'd test some of the things I've learned teaching sensuality classes." Her fingers grazed his abs and she tugged his shirt out from his khakis.

"Oh yeah?" He thought about imprisoning her hand the

next time she tried some fleeting caress. "What kind of classes involve blindfolds?"

"Being blindfolded helps make you more aware of your other senses." Slowly she unbuttoned his shirt, remaining an arm's length from him. He tried to reach for her but she danced backward, out of his reach.

"Don't you think it would be beneficial for my senses to touch you?" He wanted the feel of her against him, the scent of her hair in his nose. "Taste you?"

"Soon." She whispered the word in that husky tone and he wondered if she was afraid the neighbors would hear or if the soft voice and blindfolding were just the next steps in expanding her sexual horizons.

He could damn well get on board with that.

Shoving his shirt off his shoulders, Rocco caught a hint of her scent, something spicier than she'd worn over the weekend. Before he could reach for her, she disappeared again, leaving him swiping at air.

"Are you taking your clothes off now?"

"Do you want me to?"

"I wanted you naked five minutes ago."

She chuckled low in her throat and something soft swiped across his bare chest.

Her hair?

The fleeting touch came again and he grabbed for it, crushing a long feather in his hands.

"Tsk, tsk. Impatient man." She leaned against him, brushing the tips of her breasts across his chest where the feather had been a moment ago. He felt only creamy skin and a wisp of silky lingerie.

Air stuck in his lungs and he thought they might combust.

Unable to resist, his hands gravitated to those soft mounds, sculpting her curves to fit his palms.

Something didn't feel right.

The realization hit him in a flash, a combination of the wrong voice, the wrong scent, the wrong feel in his arms. Jesus. What if this was the wrong woman?

Muttering a curse, he released her to reach for his blindfold. He yanked it off in time to hear the woman's retreating feet. See a hint of her shadow near the front door.

"Hey!" Rocco growled the word, diving toward the foyer and running into some low piece of furniture.

Kicking aside the leather footrest, he stepped into a shot of pain up his bad ankle and heard the door close behind her. By the time he made it out of the house, his shirt off and his breath still coming fast, he could see the Escalade's taillights disappearing up the street, a new license plate on the back.

He didn't have time to read the whole thing, but he thought he caught the last two letters.

"Shit," he yelled, at no one in particular and life in general, his foot still throbbing with the aftershock of a wrong sudden move.

Once again that weakness had cost him.

Anger bubbled and he regretted not parking closer to the condo. He might have been able to catch her if he hadn't parked in the courtesy lot behind the building.

"Rocco?"

A clear and familiar feminine voice drifted on the warm spring breeze and he turned to see Jessica—the real deal Jessica—coming around the corner of the building.

Busted. Right when he needed to call the cops to chase the woman down.

He stalked toward her, forcing himself not to limp, and she quickened her step to close the distance.

"What are you doing here?" Her eyes raked his body from head to toe, lingering on his chest.

His *bare* chest, since his shirt was somewhere on the floor of her apartment along with his cell phone.

"Did you or did you not ask me to meet you here?" He was so confused he couldn't be sure who had left the voice mail. "I got a phone message—"

Her face paled and she halted on the sidewalk.

"It wasn't from me." Her dark eyes darted to the door of her apartment. "Oh God. You were in there with—her?"

"Nothing happened." He slid an arm around her and urged her toward her place so he could make the call.

"Unless you're prone to walking around my neighborhood with no shirt on, I'm going to go out on a limb and say something damn well did happen."

He could feel the hum of anger through her, its reverberation thrumming along his hand where he touched her. Crap. He'd told himself that he would easily forget about Jess's dismissal of him after they'd slept together. But now, when she seemed on the brink of telling him to go to hell for good, Rocco understood how much he didn't want that to happen.

"I THOUGHT SHE WAS YOU."

Rocco's explanation didn't do a damn thing to soothe her frayed nerves now that they were inside her apartment. He'd already phoned the police to report a breaking and entering. A squad car was on the way.

Jessica saw a crushed feather on the floor and some

massage oils lined up on a coffee table. She wanted to throw up.

Had this bitch impersonator touched Rocco in ways Jessica hadn't even thought up yet? As a woman with a career rooted in providing high-end services to high-end women, Jessica didn't indulge her inner street kid very often. But damn it, it was itching for free rein right now.

Plucking up one of the miniature bottles of oil, she saw that it was still full and sealed shut. That didn't stop her from wishing she could wind up and toss the thing against her unused fireplace. The sound of shattering glass all over the phony logs she'd shoved in there last Christmas would be damn satisfying right about now.

"Jessica, the cops will dust for fingerprints. We shouldn't touch anything until after they've had a chance to go through the whole place."

She set the bottle back down, brimming with emotions and the sense of having her physical space violated. Anger bubbled up her throat.

"Why is she doing this to me?" Her fury threatened to choke her. "How could she come here and—"

She looked Rocco up and down, her sense of betrayal growing with each passing second.

"Nothing happened." He settled his hands on her shoulders and held her at arm's length. "I thought she was you because she said she wanted to try out some sensual stuff from one of her workshops. She blindfolded me the second I walked in here, which tells me she must not look too much like you up close or I would have known right away."

She nodded, remembering Mrs. Teraza had not had her glasses on when she saw the other woman either. That didn't stop her from shaking. Her whole body quaked with tremors of panic and anger that this…woman, this…piranha had dared to threaten Jessica's world.

"Did you…kiss her?" She wished she didn't need to know all the gory details. She didn't *want* to know. But she couldn't stand *not* knowing either.

"No! Hell, no." Rocco rubbed her shoulders with his warm, strong hands. "I would have recognized your kiss. For that matter, I would have recognized the feel of you against me if she'd gotten that close, but she didn't. Well, not until I crushed the stupid feather and tried to grab her. And then I knew it wasn't you."

The mangled quill seemed to back up his story and it boded well that the massage oil hadn't been used, right? Still, the violation of this bitch in her house, touching Rocco… Helpless rage pummeled her insides.

"You took off your shirt so you must not have been totally immune."

In a perfect world, she might not harp on that. But the reality was that she could hardly contain her jealousy. Her wrath.

A police car rolled to a stop in the driveway, the sound of screeching tires and doors slamming putting an end to the conversation for the next hour while the cops combed through her whole house.

All her possessions were touched, questions were asked. She passed through the whole ordeal in a blur, answering automatically while she made coffee and tried not to get in the way.

Rocco proved much better at dealing with the police. He repeated what she had told him about the stolen files from her office and she made plans to go to the station the next morning to file a more extensive complaint. Right now she was just so damn scattered she couldn't think and she was petrified she'd leave out some critical detail that would help the police figure out why an old friend would persecute her this way.

Nearly two hours later, the police left and Rocco helped her clean up the mess. The investigators had been respectful, but their thoroughness had left things in total disarray. Finally, when the worst of it had been cleared up, Rocco caught her hands in his and halted her in the middle of the living room.

"I'm sorry, Jess. I thought it was you. I was just so damn glad you wanted to see me again."

Some of the anger that had been burning strong for the past two hours slipped away at his admission. If anything, the intensity of her feelings right now told her she wasn't ready to cut ties with Rocco. Whether or not he would ever be the kind of man capable of the deeper, emotional relationship she wanted one day, she understood now that she couldn't let him go just yet.

Perhaps there had been more between them than she'd admitted the first time.

"You thought she was me." She repeated his words, turning over that idea in her mind. "Am I so easily substituted?"

"No." He swore an oath and released her to drop-kick the crumpled feather that still lay on the floor.

That pleased her. Especially when the poor, broken quill didn't sail beyond a few inches. She smiled in spite of herself.

"Maybe I ought to make sure you never mistake anyone else for me again."

She couldn't do anything to find Leslie Ann right now. And frankly, she'd given the woman enough thought over the past few hours. Nothing mattered more to Jessica at this moment than making certain Rocco would never mistake another woman for her. She would leave her mark on him somehow.

Turning, he stared at her, anger of his own brewing in his icy blue eyes.

"And just how do you propose to do that?"

"I'm going to show you how irreplaceable I am." The more she thought about the idea, the more she liked it. Moving around the room, she switched on one light after another. "And I'm going to make sure you can see every inch of me while I'm at it."

His gaze followed her past the fireplace, where she side-stepped a fern overflowing its pot. Once she had illuminated the room with every lamp in sight, she started touching a match to the candles.

"I know what you look like."

"Not well enough to distinguish me in a room full of shadows." Her heart beat faster with the knowledge of what she wanted to do. What she hoped she could do.

"It was a one-time accident." His words had the ring of a man speaking between gritted teeth, but she refused to be deterred.

"My unwanted twin waltzed into my office and made off with my client list and God knows what else this morning. Obviously, she's fooling other people in my life."

Mrs. Teraza had offered to give a statement to the police after Jessica had called her and filled her in on the breaking and entering at her house. She would go down to the station tomorrow too.

"I'm going to help you find her, you know."

Jessica took Rocco's hand and pulled him forward, guiding him toward a leather wing chair that didn't match any of her other salvaged pieces.

"Right after this." Pushing his shoulder, she urged him down into the chair.

"Jess, you really shouldn't—"

She whipped off her top and flung it at him. The gold silk pelted him in the chest then slid down to cover his lap.

"She's shorter than me, you know. If Leslie Ann is behind all this, she's almost an inch shorter than me."

"You don't need to do this." His voice went steely, but she thought she sensed a thaw in his eyes.

Fingers sliding down the straps of her bra, she flicked one off her shoulder and then the other.

"And I used to be a little better endowed." She let the delicate lace cups roll down the swell of her breasts. "But she could have had that altered or she could have found a good padded bra."

She noticed Rocco had quit protesting and his attention seemed fixed to her body. Good.

She liked the thrill of having him there, watching her. Something about the rapt masculine attention soothed away part of the anger she felt at having had her home invaded—and Rocco—touched.

"Jess."

Her name sounded like music on his tongue, the sibilance hissed out on a long breath.

"Last I knew, she also favored men's cologne over traditional perfumes because, according to her, musk makes her horny." Unhooking the bra, she let it drop to her feet before she stepped out of her shoes and walked closer to him.

He reached for her leg but she didn't want him to touch her just yet.

"Look a little longer, will you? I won't be so forgiving the next time you confuse me with anyone else." Sliding down the zipper on her skirt, she let the fabric fall with a *swish* around her ankles.

Rocco's eyes widened at the sight of her undergarments, chosen that morning with him in mind.

She'd taken the time to dig out a pair of silk stockings—an indulgence she'd bought long ago during her early attempts to feel beautiful again. The fabric was so sheer you'd never know she had hose on just by looking at her ankles or calves. What made the stockings a visual treat were the ivory satin garters dangling from a lace belt worn over matching panties.

It was the kind of getup that must have made women of another era feel voluptuous. The lingerie was certainly working some magic for her today and, if the bulge in Rocco's khakis was any indication, the outfit worked damn well for him too.

"Lastly, Leslie used to have a tattoo on her hip." Jessica moved aside the strings tying her bikini undies around her hips to indicate the spot. "Right about here."

Bumping out her hip, she angled it so he could see.

"So where she has a rather forbidding looking barbed-wire cross, I have nothing but—" she slid the knot free to unfasten the underwear "—skin."

With a groan, Rocco reached for her, pulling her hips toward him until his lips found the flesh in question. He covered the area with his mouth and swirled his tongue around the bare skin.

Her knees weakened in response as she edged closer, only too glad for him to taste her. Fingers spearing into his hair, she held on to him and let the fire of being with Rocco burn away everything but that moment.

His teeth grazed her skin and his tongue soothed the spot. He spun her to face him, only lifting his mouth from her when one garter strap got in the way. Even then, he breathed hotly on that place, inciting a whimper. Her fingers curled helplessly on his shoulders, her body craving release even as she wanted to delay it. Savor it.

His hands worked nimbly on her clothes, untying the other knot on her panties and flicking open garter fastenings until her hips were bare and he leaned forward to cup her bottom in his hands. The high she felt made her dizzy, the idea of giving herself so completely to someone providing a head rush.

The reality of his lips between her legs melted her from the inside out. All sensation concentrated right there, right where his tongue stroked her into a frenzy.

Pleasure snowballed, gathering speed and momentum until she was powerless to stop it. She wriggled back from him, but he held her firm, continuing that relentless drive to bliss when she wanted to draw it out and make it last.

Her shout rose in her throat, reaching her mouth the same time the first wave of an orgasm swamped her. His arms climbed higher to support her as her whole body turned boneless. She twisted with each new ripple of pleasure as it washed over her again and again. The primal joy of it took her breath away and she was struck with the urge to cover this man in kisses for opening a whole new world to her.

When he released her, she sank into his lap, relishing the feel of his strong thighs beneath her quivering legs. She cupped his face in her hands, holding him steady to receive her kiss.

"Come inside me," she whispered to him as her lips brushed his. He tasted like sex.

Jessica had a vague sense of Rocco searching for a condom in his wallet and shoving off his pants, but mostly she gave herself over to the task of lavishing his neck and shoulders with small nips and licks. When he was ready for her, he lifted her high up on his chest and eased her down to meet him. The hot feel of him against her swollen sex was deliriously good and she accepted his body into hers with a quick jerk of her hips.

He tensed, impossibly hard inside her. She couldn't take him all without leaning back. Draping her legs over the arms of the chair. Only then did they fit together, bodies tense with longing.

"I can't move." She gazed up at him, her skin slick from the heat radiating off their bodies. "There's not enough room."

She didn't think she could sit up and still take all of him. Not now, when she was a mass of tingling nerve endings.

"You can dance for me. Right here." He moved her hips with his hands. "Like in the class you taught."

She smiled, discovering yet another facet of sex with Rocco. Fun. Right now, after a day filled with betrayal and violation, she desperately needed the escape that fun provided.

"I don't know if I can, but I want to." She arched her back and rolled her hips, and a groan wrenched free from his throat.

"Clearly you're plenty capable." His words were taut with strain as she moved against him.

Delighting in this new power over him, she contracted her abs, flexing them in time to an unheard rhythm. Over and over she rode the thick length of him, mindless with the feel of it until he rose right out of the chair, taking her with him. He wrapped her around him easily, holding her in his arms until he reached a wall.

"My turn," he whispered, cradling her thighs while the wall supported her back.

Then he set up a rhythm all his own, a relentless drive that told her he'd been in charge all along. She sank into what he wanted, clinging to his broad shoulders while her body answered his.

This was what *she* wanted. What they both needed. And he'd managed to give it to her without ever pinning her beneath him.

The realization hit her the same time as her second orgasm. The simple tenderness he'd shown her flashed through her head like a news bulletin while she unraveled in his arms. He joined her a split second after, his powerful body tensing and shuddering while she tried to come to terms with what had just happened.

Rocco had slid past her defenses like a true SEAL, with covert maneuvers that minimized confrontation. He'd won her body over with consummate skill.

And as much as she'd like to linger in sensual oblivion in the arms of a man who never let his guard down,

Jessica feared the repo man posed a larger threat than the military guy.

Because if she wasn't careful, she had the feeling Rocco would steal off with her heart one night…and she might never get it back.

_11_

"THAT'S IT? That's all you can do?"

Jessica looked back and forth between two cops that Rocco guessed would be undressing her with their eyes if he wasn't standing a few feet away.

Their trip to the local cop shop had been a bust, although Jessica had certainly provided a few thrills for the guys on duty between the illustrated copy of the Kama Sutra that had fallen out of her bag and her natural ability to turn heads. But the joys in this trip were all one-sided since the police had told her they hadn't found any signs of Leslie Ann James despite running the partial plate number Rocco remembered and an APB on the Escalade since it now had stolen plates.

They'd gotten here before nine in the morning, both ready to flee the warmth of intimacy hanging over her apartment after they awoke wrapped in each other's arms. He'd brewed the coffee while she showered and they were out of the house a half hour later, each content to retreat to their own corner.

"We'll send someone over to the address you gave us in Chula Vista again and see if there are any signs she's come back." The younger of the two guys at the desk gestured to the notes he'd made on Jessica's statement while the older one peeled away to help a foreign couple who'd just walked in.

"But I told you, we drove by that address on our way here this morning and there's a For Rent sign out front. She knew we found her and now she's gone."

Rocco had been beyond pissed to see the empty garage and a realty company's lockbox on the door. Leslie Ann James looked guiltier by the second, but without any concrete leads to her whereabouts, the cops couldn't do much more than be on alert for when she showed up again. Rocco's father hadn't been happy about the lost vehicle, but at least he'd sounded sharper this morning when Rocco had phoned him.

"Ma'am, that's why we recommend the general public shouldn't get involved with police affairs—"

Jessica's whole posture changed, her body tensing as if she would launch over the desk if she didn't hold herself back.

"I've reported every step of this problem starting Friday night when my vehicle was nearly repossessed because of this mix-up. Monday I brought you the tape of her using my name to buy the vehicle, and today I'm telling you she stole my office files by waltzing into my workplace and pretending to be me. Can you tell me *when* this is going to become a police affair?"

"Jess." Rocco thought he'd better intervene before she ticked off the people who could best help her.

The older cop had stopped listening to the foreign couple who'd apparently had some traveler's checks stolen. A few guys in the cubicles behind the main desk turned to look their way.

"No, I want to know. Every time I've spoken to this department, I've been told that you either can't, won't, or don't foresee yourselves helping me with the matter. So at what point did this become police business?"

The cop she'd been addressing didn't look so smitten with her anymore. His face flushed as he lowered his voice.

"It's been police business from the first day, but the unfortunate reality of police work is that we've got gangbangers and child molesters posing more of a threat than your look-alike friend here. I suggest you go home, and we'll call you when we have a lead."

She nodded woodenly and Rocco steered her out of there, knowing he could help her if she'd let him. He might not be a cop, but he hadn't worked on covert military operations for the better part of a decade without learning a few things about tracking down people who didn't want to be found.

When they reached the exit and headed back out onto the street she rounded on him.

"If no one cares that I'm being impersonated or that my clients' privacy has been compromised, I have to at least go to work and do some damage control." She wound a series of curls around her finger from a ponytail that didn't begin to contain her hair.

She'd dressed for business today—a black suit with a fitted black silk tank underneath. Still, the short skirt and low square cut of the tank was sexy as hell. She sported heavy tortoiseshell eyeglasses, too, which he'd learned were all for show since she had perfect vision.

"I can help you find her." He walked toward his truck. He'd given her a ride to the station and she lived close enough to the precinct for him to easily drop her back at her apartment now, but he hoped he could talk her into his plan.

"Why? So you can get your father's vehicle back and I can get yelled at by cops who may or may not do anything about her?" She dropped the lock of hair she'd been holding and shook her head. "I'll report this latest news to the insurance investigator and see what he has to say. My business insurance rep wasn't too keen on someone using my credit to purchase an extra vehicle, so maybe they'll step up—"

"Do what you want, but I'm not willing to let it go. I would have pursued you all over the state to retrieve my father's vehicle and I plan to do the same with this Leslie chick." They reached his pickup truck and he held the door wide. "But if this hasn't crossed a line for you or felt a little too personal yet, then go home and don't worry about it. There's no sense borrowing trouble if you can avoid it."

Pausing with one foot on the running board, she shook her head.

"You know damn well it feels personal to me." She clutched her papers so tightly in one arm that the corners wrinkled and the Kama Sutra book threatened to escape all over again.

"Then it's up to you if you want to pursue a matter the police told you to stay out of or not. But either way, I'm going to recommend you don't stay alone at your apartment for a while."

"Why?" Climbing into the passenger seat, she presented him with a tempting rear view. "If she tries to come back to my place, I'll call the cops faster than she can say *busted*."

Rocco closed the door before jogging around to his side of the truck and climbing into the driver's seat.

"This woman is getting damn ballsy by impersonating you to people who know you. What if she hopes to *become* you?"

That got her attention. Jessica swung on him, eyes wide.

"What's that supposed to mean?"

"Jess, think about it. She knows everything about you and she's fooled multiple people with her act." He kept coming back to the impersonation factor since run-of-the-mill identity theft didn't require such a level of high drama. "What's to stop her from bumping you off and basically stepping right into your shoes and taking over your life?"

She whipped off her eyeglasses and massaged her temple.

"That's crazy."

"Yeah well, it was damn crazy to try and seduce me in your house, but that didn't stop her from trying."

Jessica glared at him across the truck cab, with no eyewear to impede the laser focus of her gaze.

"All right, Sherlock, I'll bite. What exactly did you have in mind for hunting down this chick on our own?"

THERE WAS REGULAR crazy and then there was "out of your mind" type crazy. Jessica feared Rocco had overstepped that boundary.

She waited for him in the cab of his truck, a block down from Leslie Ann's old house, now up for rent. On the way over here, he'd spelled out a scheme so underhanded she'd almost nixed it. But it was so damn clever she couldn't help but be intrigued. And they weren't technically doing anything illegal.

Just lying in spades.

Punching in another number on Rocco's cell phone,

she called the local library in Chula Vista, using the phone book he'd left in her lap while he went to work on the street outside the vacated house. The plan was for her to pretend to be, well, herself, while she called local businesses to see what other damage Leslie Ann might have done while using her name. Of course, if that didn't work, she was supposed to use Leslie's name on the next round of phone calls to find out if anyone might know a forwarding address.

So far, the video stores and the dry cleaners had no record of a Jessica Winslow. For the call to the library, Jessica decided to use Leslie's name.

The phone rang and rang as she watched Rocco speak to an attractive young woman jogging with two dogs outside Leslie's old place. The runner had buns of steel, her tight pink workout wear highlighting every square inch of her bod.

Since when was she the jealous type?

"Have you been helped?" An impatient voice on the other end of the phone kept Jessica from flying out of the truck to wrap herself around Rocco.

And where did all that possessiveness come from?

"Yes," she lied. "I'm Leslie Ann James and I was holding for the person who was going to tell me the last few books I checked out. I forgot to make the notations for my bibliography."

Rocco had spoon-fed her a handful of gimmicks on the way over to Chula Vista, his half-hour brief on intelligence gathering stirring hope that they might be able to find Leslie yet.

Before she committed more identity fraud with the client information she stole. Or before she took over

Jessica's life while removing Jessica from it. Neither option pleased her, but the threat to her client information seemed a bit more preferable in light of Rocco's other theory.

"James, you say?" The woman let out a long-suffering sigh. "I don't see anything by that name."

"Perhaps someone misfiled it?" She forced a nervous laugh, remembering the way Rocco had explained that people were more apt to help someone they thought was in dire straits. "I'm so sorry, but I've got the meanest professor you can imagine and I know she'll give me an F—"

Another sigh. "What's the street address?"

Jessica reeled off the numbers as Rocco and the runner parted ways up the street. She noticed the pink dog-walking parade had turned around to scope out Rocco's butt as she departed, and it occurred to Jessica that she'd never had to deal with jealousy since she'd done so little dating. How would it feel to be with a man who women so clearly salivated over?

"Leslie Ann James Baylock. Did you marry or divorce recently?"

At the mention of the last name, Jessica froze. Her brain seized up.

"Excuse me?"

"We have it under Baylock, so it was darn lucky I was able to call up the record at all. Are you ready for the book information? I can only give you title and author though, because we're swamped. You can get whatever else you want off the Internet."

Jessica plucked up the pen sandwiched between the pages of the phone book and fumbled for a piece of paper, her fingers not working quite right.

Leslie Ann James was using the last name of Jessica's long-ago rapist. Baylock.

"I'm d-divorced, by the way," she stammered finally to answer the woman's earlier question. "I've been doing my best to forget him."

The lady on the other end cackled between quick snaps of chewing gum.

"Good for you honey. You borrowed *Making the IRS Work for You* and *Must-Have Tax Credits*." She rattled off the authors as Rocco arrived back at the truck.

Thanking the woman, Jessica disconnected the call and hoped she wouldn't spew her breakfast.

"What is it?" Rocco frowned as soon as he opened the passenger door.

Jessica swallowed, knowing she couldn't avoid the memories she'd swept under the rug too many times.

"She's going by Leslie Baylock." It took a Herculean effort not to spit when she said it, but the name didn't mean squat to Rocco. "The surname is significant. It's shared by the bastard who attacked me when I was seventeen."

ROCCO HADN'T known what to say when Jessica revealed her identity thief's sick use of a last name. And now, after a few hours of phone calls and questions back at his house, he still didn't know quite how to offer her comfort. He was better at direct confrontation than dealing with the emotional fallout afterward, but at least now he had a few more concrete facts to offer her.

He hoped that would help erase the hunted look in her eyes that had cropped up while they were in Chula Vista. The bone-deep fear was something he'd seen before in victims of war. And just once in his mother's eyes when she'd been diagnosed in the late stages of her cancer. He'd seen the same fear echoed in his father's eyes that day, but nothing could have prepared him to see the look in Jess's face. Not when he'd started caring for her more than he had any right to.

He hung up the phone from his latest call to a Colorado records department and left his office to see where Jessica had retreated.

She hadn't put up much of a protest about staying at his place for a few days even though he knew that kind of enforced intimacy would freak her out a little. They'd both been rattled after she spent the night and they'd never really addressed why. Jessica had simply asked for space and he'd given it without so much as a discussion. Then, after her impersonator tried to seduce him...well, they'd both been too tightly wound to think through what they were doing.

"Jessica?" He found her on the back porch, a deep swath of roof-shaded tiles that ran along the length of the house.

She sat in an old porch swing made of salvaged split-rails. Perched in one corner of the swing, she had a piece of paper in her hand and a skinny calico cat he'd never seen before curled up against her thigh.

"I'm just reading a thank-you note I received from one of my workshop attendees last weekend." She waved the piece of paper. "Bryanna was one of the women who found you in the hallway that first night and she e-mailed to tell me that she convinced her husband to go into marriage counseling after she completed the workshop. I hope it works out for her."

"That's great." Rocco let the screen door bang behind

him. "It seemed like all the women who showed up for your classes were really focused on what you had to say. Your material obviously appealed to them."

A ghost of a smile flashed around her lips, and then it disappeared.

"Did you find out anything?" She pulled the cat into her arms, the printed e-mail falling to one side.

"Possibly." He sat beside her on the swing that he'd never had reason to use up until now. He wasn't exactly the kind of guy to kick back and drink beer on the porch on Sundays.

"I don't understand. Either you discovered something or you didn't, right?" Her hand stroked down the calico's fur again and again and he got the idea the cat was soothing her rather than the other way around.

"The information I got came from documents and court records, and you know—after I nearly repossessed your vehicle—that documents can lie." He didn't want to upset her unnecessarily so he thought it wise to lay some groundwork for his revelations.

And damn but he hoped he could scavenge up the right words.

"What do the records show, Rocco?" She lowered her voice. "I promise I can handle it."

His eyes roamed over her and he realized she could take whatever life dished out. She'd already been through hell.

"It looks like your friend Leslie married Scott Baylock." He'd double-checked the names and addresses multiple times to be sure, tracing Leslie's movements back to when she'd lived next door to her during Jessica's stint in a foster home.

Her gasp scared the cat right off the swing.

"And here's the kicker. She didn't start using the married

name until after she dropped out of college, but she's got a marriage license on file in Kentucky dating back to the summer she turned eighteen."

He handed over the piece of paper he'd had faxed to him under the pretense that his kid was working on a genealogy project.

Jessica's eyes scanned the paper as she reached for a can of iced tea on the floor at her feet.

"She turned eighteen the same summer I was assaulted." She stopped reading to look off into the distance. "If the paper is accurate, she would have had to have taken off for Kentucky just before the bastard attacked me."

He took the paper back and stuffed it into his shirt pocket while she gulped a long drink. Was she handling the news well? She wasn't shaking and she hadn't cried. But the betrayal had to cut much deeper than the identity theft.

"Can you think of any reason why she would do something like that to you while pretending to be your friend?"

She rounded on him. "Other than being pure, undiluted evil?"

"She must have wanted some kind of friendship with you if she moved from Colorado to attend college with you even if it was only for a year."

"Maybe she felt guilty she'd held me while I sobbed my eyes out over a rape committed by the same son of a bitch she'd been married to all along—"

Her words broke then, any facade of handling the news vanishing as her lips moved and no sound issued forth. She gestured vaguely with her hand before the tears came in earnest.

Compassion for her, for what she'd been through, made

Rocco pull her into his arms and hold her while she cried. Compassion made him rub her spine and kiss the back of her head through the veil of her hair.

But alongside the compassion, he experienced an upwelling of rage so fierce he could hardly sit still. He could find the guy who had done this to her and make him disappear. He'd been trained by the best to kill quickly and efficiently and he'd never in his life been so tempted to use that knowledge for personal purposes.

"Didn't they put out a warrant for his arrest, Jess? If I could find traces of him this fast, the cops had to have been able to track him down." How could the police have dropped the ball on a case involving a minor?

"They told me he disappeared." She sniffled, but her tears seemed to have slowed. "I did the testing and had the rape kit, but he left no traces behind so it would have been my word against his anyway. The police said he was a transient and I—as long as I didn't have to see him, I told myself that would have to be good enough."

Swiping away the last of the tear streaks on her face, she sat up and straightened her shoulders.

He didn't want to jab a gaping wound any more than he had to, so he let the matter of Baylock ride for now. Besides, he had so many questions about the wife he hardly knew where to begin.

"Were you aware that Baylock and your friend even knew each other the summer they supposedly married?" No matter how he juggled the pieces, he couldn't make them fit. That bothered him and with each passing second, he became more certain he would locate Baylock himself and ensure judgment was passed.

If he couldn't find a way to wear a badge by then so he could do it the legal way, he would indulge his inner vigilante and drag the prick in by his toenails.

"Yes." Jessica jumped off the swing and paced the porch. "Actually, it was Leslie who introduced me to Scott. We ran into him on the street one day."

"Jesus—"

"Afterward, I believed her when she said how much she regretted it and how she barely knew him and never would have guessed he'd be that kind of guy." Her brow scrunched in thought, her long legs coming to a stop. "And, looking back, she must have put on a hell of a convincing show, because she seemed genuinely sorry."

But Rocco had heard all he could take of Leslie Ann James Baylock's phony bullshit for one day. It occurred to him that maybe Jessica wasn't any better at reading people than he if she'd allowed this woman to get so close to her. They'd both been taken in by pros.

Rising from the swing, his hands gravitated to Jessica's shoulders, needing to touch her.

"We're not going to find any answers beating our heads against a wall. You closed your credit card accounts earlier and you've frozen your business accounts until further notice. You've done all you can for tonight."

She nodded, seeming to understand even if she didn't agree. He knew how much it bothered her that someone close to her could turn out to be so cold, a feeling he identified with all too well.

That thought reminded him why he kept relationships simple. Uncomplicated. Easy to walk away from.

Until now.

Shacking up with Jessica, even on a temporary basis, would only entwine their lives all the more.

"The cops will come up with something. Her prints will match a past crime or they'll turn up a forwarding address. Either way, we'll find her and her prick of a husband, too." He stroked a hand through her hair and wondered about the best strategy for going to bed.

Haul her to his like he wanted to? Or would that be as good as admitting he had no control over his desire for her?

"I just hope we hear something soon."

The worry in her voice would melt all his honorable intentions if he didn't retreat from her in a hurry.

"We will." Releasing her shoulders with an effort, Rocco took a deep breath of fresh air to chase the scent of her from his nose. "And in the meantime, I'm going to make a few more calls and see if I can learn anything about him. You should come in and get some sleep."

Peeling himself away from her had to be one of the hardest things he'd ever done, but in the interest of self-preservation, he held the door and waited as she stepped inside.

Away from him and the persistent longings of his heart.

12

LESLIE SERIOUSLY CONTEMPLATED the carving block full of knives on the kitchen counter when she heard a car pull in the driveway.

If Scott killed her, it would be a long drawn out process and he would make sure she was thoroughly humiliated first. He'd changed so much since she'd fallen in love with him all those years ago. Or maybe he'd always been on a mountain of a power trip and he'd just hidden it from her better in the old days. He constantly reminded her of the hell he'd saved her from by marrying her, and it was true that Scott had seemed like an angel compared to her abusive father. But did he have to play his wives against one another so cruelly?

Peering out into the driveway, Leslie saw him. Scott had come alone to wreak whatever vengeance he was in the mood for today. He'd been pissed that he had to get rid of the Escalade prematurely, but she knew they needed to get it over the border in a hurry if they wanted to make any money off it.

Of course, after she'd explained why the Escalade had to go immediately, she'd had no choice but to admit she also needed to move locations and get out of Chula Vista.

Scott would have gone ballistic if he couldn't find her at the old place, and he visited her faithfully once every five nights when it was her turn to have him. He used to show up once every fourth night, but in addition to his wives, he'd recently brought home a young runaway for Leslie to coax into the family. That had been the first time Leslie cut herself. She felt sorry for the girl; what could she offer the scared young woman when Scott had already taken her innocence and wouldn't let her contact her family?

The religious rewards of their lifestyle had become a hard sell now that Scott didn't obey any of the teachings he had once preached to them so devoutly.

"What in the hell has gotten into you, Leslie Ann?" He stomped into the kitchen as if he owned the place, as if it wasn't the first time he'd set foot in the new house she'd rented under an assumed name.

She wished she didn't still love him. At six foot two, he had the body of an athlete thanks to the tennis he played every day at a local country club. She was the only one of his wives he took there. His public wife.

His hair was impeccably cut, his dress pants crisp despite the long drive from the family's home base.

"Well?" He pounded his fist against the tiny island in the duplex's kitchen, making the knives inside the carving block rattle from the vibration.

Indignant over his attitude when she was earning the living for a family that would strap any legitimate working person's wallet, she met him toe to toe.

"I've had a lot to do this week, Scott. I can't just rush in and steal a database and snatch Jessica at the same time without anyone noticing." She'd had to do a week's worth of work in a day to waltz into Jess's office and make off with the sensitive information and a pile of rich women's credit card numbers. "Did I mention she has a boyfriend watching her every move now?"

That got his attention.

"What are you talking about?" His dark eyes flared with palpable jealousy. She took malicious pleasure from hurting him even as it twisted an old knife inside her that he cared so much about someone else.

She had been the first to date him. First in his bed. But Jessica Winslow had been first in his thoughts for years afterward. Leslie had shed bitter tears that she'd ever introduced them.

"When she saw me on the street that day, she was with a guy." A hot, sexy former SEAL, she'd found out after a little research on the stud she'd played blindfold games with today.

A stupid risk that had cost her, but maybe in some tiny recess of her heart, she wanted to be caught. Wanted Scott to know she wasn't completely under his thumb anymore. Maybe that's why she didn't bother telling Scott her new home backed up to the acreage that Rocco Easton owned in Dulzura. She'd rented it knowing the fence protecting the perimeter of his property bordered some woods behind this duplex.

"I thought she never dated." Scott turned away from her, his eyes darting around the kitchen without really seeing anything. "You said she kept to herself. That she focused all her time and energies on this business of hers."

He cracked his knuckles, a habit that annoyed her. The methodical flexing of his joints until they popped had precipitated him punching things enough times that the noise made her want to run for cover.

"All of which was true until this past week. She must have met him very recently."

He muttered under his breath something that sounded like "slut" and she wondered if Jessica's boyfriend could be the thing that finally tarnished her for Scott. A thrill shot through her at the thought.

"We have to bring her into the family now. Tomorrow." He spun on his heel and pinned her with eyes that looked a little feral, still massaging his knuckles. "Where are her clients' credit card numbers? I have a buyer ready for them tonight and a carrier waiting who can take the information over the border for me."

Right this minute, he almost sounded like his old self, full of drive and purpose and making things happen for the family. So what if he'd lost all his religious convictions? Leslie had never been in it for her soul's salvation. All she'd ever wanted was to be Scott's favorite wife, the love of his life.

Leslie's hands shook with new purpose and hope. He'd called Jessica a slut—the most derogatory insult this particular man could possibly hurl.

"Great." She retrieved a flash drive with the database from her purse. "After your meeting with the carrier, we can talk about how you want me to handle Jessica."

She debated telling him they could pick her up tonight. With a little ingenuity, they could get through the fencing around the property to steal her away as soon as Scott returned. Would he be happy with Leslie then?

With a terse nod, he took the keys, seeming to agree to

all her plans. She'd almost forgotten the thrill of being first in Scott's thoughts.

The woman he needed more than any other.

"And if Jessica can't be coaxed into the family or if her boyfriend's pull proves too great, I'll bet we can unload her in Mexico, too."

She'd meant it as a joke. Well, sort of as a joke.

But she could see the error in her judgment almost immediately as Scott's fist cocked back. As for the punch itself, she never saw it coming.

"I CAN'T GO to sleep."

Jessica resisted the urge to grab Rocco by the front of his T-shirt and drag him into the house with her, but it wasn't easy. She needed him. Here. With her. Desperately.

"You'll be safe here." He nodded toward the house, his pale eyes catching the moonlight flooding half the porch as it rose over the tree line. "You can go in and play Pac-Man if you're not tired. I'll just be out here making some calls. I have a few cop friends I might be able to tap for help."

That wasn't what she wanted but she didn't know how to express it without appearing needy. Which, of course, she was. But damn it, her whole world had imploded over the past few days between the identity theft, her friend's betrayal and the reappearance of someone she'd never, ever wanted to see again.

"I'm sure I'll be fine," she lied, her feet moving back onto the porch instead of into the house like she knew he wanted. "I just wonder if we talked a little longer maybe we'd figure out a motive or a connection to my past we're not seeing."

It seemed like a brilliant point to her, but he shook it off right away.

"You're exhausted and you've thought about this stuff too much today already. You'll be more clearheaded tomorrow and we can see what you come up with then."

Panic fluttered in her chest, drying up her throat and setting her heart into manic overdrive. Her brain searched for the right words to convince him they needed to stay together and came up hopelessly blank. She needed him to hold her. To wrap his big gorgeous body around her and keep bad dreams at bay until she found her feet again.

Rocco opened the door to the house again, as if he fully expected her to simply agree to the plan. When she still didn't move, he put two fingers in his mouth and let out a long whistle.

"You haven't even met the dogs yet. Wait until you see these two. They're sweet as pups to friends, but they'll tear the hide off of anyone who tries to get in here." On cue, two giant, long-haired animals bounded out of the woods on one side of the house. "I'm telling you, you've got every reason to rest easy."

Jessica petted them both, on autopilot, while Rocco introduced the Akidas—Molly and Maggie.

"It's not that I'm afraid of something happening to me," she admitted finally, hoping that a dose of complete honesty would make him stay with her.

"It's okay, Jess." He quit scratching Molly and stood. "Anyone would be rattled after the day you've had. You've got every right to be nervous."

Oh God, she'd have to go out on a limb if she wanted

him to hold her again. She'd have to turn her heart inside out, expose herself in ways she'd never considered before.

"I'm—" She pinched the bridge of her nose, as if that could hold back the flood of emotions churning just below the surface. "I wonder if you could at least…hold me until I fall asleep?"

Tears burned the back of her eyes, but she'd already cried once today and didn't want to experience another milligram of heartache over Baylock.

Compassion lit Rocco's eyes and she hated that she'd had to play that card to make him stay, but she'd had no choice. Tomorrow she'd be stronger. Tomorrow she could let him walk away and she'd fight her battle with the police and the betraying Baylocks. Tonight, she needed Rocco no matter the cost.

"Hell." He drew her into his chest, folding her against him. "This was a shit day for you."

Nodding, her face rubbed the soft cotton of his T-shirt, absorbing the scent of the warm man beneath it. His heart thumped a steady, easy rhythm under her ear.

"Of course I'll hold you. I just thought—when something goes wrong, I tend to want to go out and fix it and I thought I might be able to dig up something more tonight."

She understood. She had the sense that right and wrong were very clear to Rocco and that he would work hard to make sure anything falling on the wrong side was fixed, addressed, or brought to justice. They'd met because it wasn't enough for him to impound her car. He'd wanted to see her suffer for the deception that he thought she had committed.

Would he see any shades of right and wrong in Leslie when he caught up with her? As much as Jessica resented the woman for touching Rocco, she wondered if her former friend had been corrupted in some way by Scott. After all, Leslie hadn't exactly come from an easy background herself, and she'd married at a ridiculously young age.

"Maybe you can just fix it tomorrow since the police already know everything we know." She smoothed her fingers along his bicep, never lifting her head from the warm place she'd made for herself against his chest.

The dogs circled their legs, their nails tapping the tile floor while they lingered to see if more attention was forthcoming.

"You want to go inside?" He leaned back to peer at her in the moonlight, his face cast in shadow. "I've got another cool spot I want to show you."

"You think you can top the video game room?" She followed him inside, keeping hold of his hand in the darkness.

"It depends on your mood." He flipped on a light switch and pulled her away from the video game side of the house.

Away from the bedroom.

He entered a breezeway that led…out to the garage?

"You're taking me to see your car collection?"

She stepped into the most immaculate garage she'd ever seen, complete with some sort of rubberized floor and endless stainless steel shelving. He had an old Mustang in there, along with a shiny tow truck and a motorcycle that she thought was a vintage Harley based on a similar model her father had once "borrowed" for a few days.

"Not the cars." Rocco led her to the back of the room where a steel ladder hugged one wall. "Come on up."

Wary of climbing into heaven knows where, she let him go first, watching as he pushed open a door over his head and disappeared into a shadowy realm above her.

Following his lead, she gripped the rungs one by one and lifted herself into a low-ceilinged second story where Rocco waited in the dark, a bundle of something under one arm.

"We're almost there." He pushed on a window to his right, elbowing his way out onto a flat roof over the breezeway. Moonlight flooded the spot, obviously a new addition, since the shingles were different from the more traditional stucco on the rest of the house's roof.

Rocco spread a blanket over the flat expanse and gestured for her to take a seat.

"You can check out the view while I get us some chow. I've got a fridge in the garage." His voice faded as he disappeared back down the ladder.

Leaving her alone on a rooftop in a Southern California border town. Jessica made herself comfortable on the blanket, which was actually a well-worn sleeping bag. Did he ever sleep out here? She could see why he'd want to. The stars were amazing, cluttering the sky with layers and layers of tiny lights since there were no city lights to compete with them. In the distance, she could see a wind farm on a far hill, but there wasn't much in the way of other houses. Or maybe they just weren't lit up at night.

She could spot some of the outbuildings on Rocco's property. Another garage. The stable she'd checked out the first time she came. An old train caboose. The whole place was like a kid's fantasy home between the video games and the vehicles. Horses and four-wheelers. Dogs and trucks.

"I hope you're hungry." Rocco reappeared carrying what looked like a cement bucket. He pulled out a loaf of

French bread, two knives, a hunk of brie and some pastrami, followed by a bottle of wine and two beers. "Take your pick on the beverage."

He dropped down onto the sleeping bag beside her, the moonlight spilling over the foraged food.

"You keep wine in the garage?" She eyed the vintage more carefully, curious what kind of vino a repo man kept in his minifridge.

Rocco Easton was full of surprises.

"It's been in there since a friend brought it over to christen the tow truck six months ago, so I can't vouch for the quality." He passed her a corkscrew and a paper cup, his arm brushing hers.

A rush of hot blood through her veins told her she wanted Rocco to do more than just hold her tonight.

"You christened your tow truck?"

"Yeah. It's The Hellion, a nod to the helo squadron that picked me up after the landmine accident."

"They saved you." Her mouth went dry at the thought of what might have happened if those helo guys hadn't been close by.

"I sent them a photo of the truck after I got the name painted on. The guys were pretty pumped."

As she twisted off the cork, something about drinking wine from paper cups on a repo man's rooftop felt strangely right. The moment settled around her with a sweet warmth she'd never experienced in her months of working her butt off to afford the Escalade or any of the other high-end, superficial trappings in her life. She'd surrounded herself with luxury and nice things to feel like she'd put her poor past behind her. And Rocco's sprawl-

ing acreage and cool accumulation of worldly toys told her
he wasn't a poor man. Yet he lived without pretense, em-
bracing simple things that made him happy. She admired
that. Admired him.

And, oh Lord, who was she kidding? She felt a whole
lot more for this man than admiration. As she set aside the
cork and poured two cups full of pinot grigio, she couldn't
hold back the feelings pouring out of her just as fast. A soft
swell of emotion rose in her throat as she held out a cup to
Rocco in the moonlight.

He'd given her back her sexual confidence. Championed
her cause when the police had turned her away. And he
wasn't scared off by the fact that she'd been a rape victim
when it had sent two old boyfriends screaming for the hills
as if she had a skull-and-crossbones sign painted on her
forehead.

He grinned at her as he took the cup, clearly oblivious
to the way she was falling for him. Big-time.

13

"CHEERS TO cheap wine and starry nights." Rocco tapped his cup against Jessica's, unsure of her mood and even less sure what she wanted from him tonight.

"Cheers." Jessica sipped her wine and seemed lost in thought.

Which was fine, since she'd told him outright she needed a warm body tonight. Someone to hold her until she fell asleep. He'd like to think she needed him, not just anyone, but he would never be naive about a gorgeous woman again.

Besides, Jessica had made serious tracks away from the ranch the last time she'd been here. She might need him tonight, but he knew damn well that didn't mean she'd need him tomorrow.

"What made you leave the service?"

Her softly spoken question turned the pinot on his tongue sour.

"It's not exactly dinner conversation." He picked up the loaf of bread and sliced off a couple of hunks along with some cheese.

"There's a shooting star." She pointed out a spot in the sky in time for him to see a trail of green light before it faded. "I think it could be a good omen. But I understand if you don't want to talk about the past."

With her gentle acceptance, he would feel like an ass if he didn't tell her. Not that she had necessarily meant to corner him. Damn it, he'd never been good at reading women. Growing up with just his father had made him well versed in guy talk and totally illiterate in chick-speak.

He crammed in a few bites of pastrami for sustenance, figuring his problems would at least give her something to think about besides the bastard who'd raped her and then sicced his wife on her to steal her identity. He still wondered if there was more to the story than she'd confided. But how could he convince her to spill every secret if he didn't share something of himself in return?

"The short version is that the lower half of my leg was pretty badly fractured in a land mine explosion." He refilled his cup and added a little more wine to hers. "My foot was reconstructed, but not well enough to qualify for the SEAL teams anymore and I was too bitter to consider some desk job."

He couldn't have physically shrugged it off if he wanted to. His whole body still tensed up at what one night's stupidity had cost him. It had taken him months to walk without a limp, and sometimes when he was exhausted, the hitch in his step came back. His father had been just as devastated as he after the accident, a fact that had made Rocco think about whose dream he was living.

"So you decided to become a recovery agent." She stretched her legs out in front of her, her toes hanging over the edge of the blanket to rest on bare shingles.

"Or a cop." He didn't know quite why he tossed that out

there. Maybe he just wanted to hear her opinion. Everyone else in his life considered repo work just a step above digging ditches for a living.

"You'd make a kick-ass cop." She grinned and he couldn't deny a twinge of disappointment that her vote put him in a uniform with a badge too. "But what about the long version of the story? I don't have anywhere to go. I'm holed up behind fences and killer dogs until Scott Baylock can be arrested."

He'd stopped at her place before coming out here, and Jessica had traded her suit for more simple stuff. Jeans. A T-shirt with some kind of fairy or winged angel. He'd been too busy checking out her curves in the T-shirt to recall the pattern.

Now, as she stargazed on his sleeping bag a mere arm's length away, a slice of bare midriff showed where her shirt had ridden up. The urge to lick that patch of skin would have been overwhelming even if he didn't want to end this conversation ASAP.

"Okay." He dropped the knife back into the bucket along with the remnants of the food, tearing his focus from her skin. "The long version involves my idiocy in dating while overseas."

"Is that against the rules?" She swept aside her hair, putting the whole mass in front of one shoulder.

"Yes. No." He shook his head. "It's frowned on and it's tricky. But we're usually never involved in any one mission for so long that it presents a problem."

He should have had better self-control, a stronger ability to deny himself.

"So what happened?"

"We were sitting idle for a month, waiting for—" He didn't know how to tell the story since he couldn't reveal most of the stuff that pertained to the teams. "We needed the thumbs-up for a mission and it just wasn't coming. The guys got restless. I got restless. And on a weekend when we were cleared for the next twelve hours, I propositioned an American woman who was overseas with an engineering firm."

Traitors came in all shapes, sizes and races. The blue-eyed engineering dynamo from West Texas had turned out to have a taste for espionage.

"Did she hurt you?" Jessica rolled onto her side, propping her head with her elbow.

"She ended up propositioning *me* and it sure as hell wasn't for sex. She thought she was being sly asking me for information about our assignment, but her questions were so well-informed I knew she had to have access to extremely secure intel." He'd bolted before he even had his pants zipped, knowing he needed to get back on base before the twelve hours were up in case they were tasked to complete the assignment earlier. As far as he could tell, the mission had been compromised and it couldn't happen.

"So how did you end up by a land mine?" Jessica inched closer to him, her hips within easy reach at a time when he wanted to lose himself in her more than ever.

As if his memory—once told—could be finished and somehow put away.

"I walked home the way I knew would be fastest. The field had been swept for mines a few months earlier, but some rebels must have snuck explosives in afterward. The tree that hit my foot probably saved my life, but I wasn't in the mood for counting blessings for a hell of a long time afterward."

"What happened to the engineer lady? Were you able to let anyone know the mission was compromised?"

"The mission was survivable even though I was unconscious when it happened. The engineer has been a guest of the U.S. government since." He wouldn't tell her how cooked in betrayal the pretty Texan had been.

"You sure can pick 'em." She gave him a lopsided smile, her fingers scratching along his chest.

"Obviously, I can't." He'd had a hard time forgiving himself even though no lives were lost because of the short time he'd spent in the company of the gorgeous traitor. "My brief contact with her could have had devastating consequences."

Her eyebrows rose. "Almost every action we take in life can have devastating consequences if you want to trace it back far enough. I chose to go out on a date with a rapist and I'll never be the same again. I chose the wrong roommate in college, and it's having a really crappy effect on my here and now."

"Those situations are different. You were young. You weren't in…a critical place in the world and trained to do a job without error."

Her hand splayed on his chest, her fingers tense as she leaned in so close he could see her pupils in the moonlight.

"I've lived in San Diego long enough to be familiar with the SEAL lure and to know what's expected of you guys. And while I admire that ideal, no living, breathing man can achieve nonstop perfection even if he's trained for it. To live in that world, you have to take selective risks to maintain your focus and do your job. A night to blow off steam. A day off to get wildly drunk and make friends with the other guys." She shrugged. "The feel of a woman after a long dry spell."

He had ten arguments ready for her, but she placed a finger over his lips and pressed gently.

"You don't have to agree. Just think about it. You'd all be on antidepressants if you didn't tap an occasional release valve."

Jessica had grossly oversimplified it. Then again, the simplicity resonated with a commonsense truth he hadn't really considered. Of all the ways his friends had tried to help him feel better, to convince him he hadn't committed so heinous an act, Jessica's clear-eyed assessment brought him a small measure of comfort no one else had managed.

What had made him ever think he could stay away from her tonight?

"You're awfully damn wise for a sex expert, you know that?" He skimmed his knuckles down her cheek and cupped her chin.

"And you sure can change a subject in a hurry." In spite of her accusation, she inched her hips closer to his.

The sleeping bag wadded up between them, the fabric catching on the shingles.

He tugged the neck of her T-shirt wide so he could plant kisses along her collarbone. The constant winds blowing across the dry hills made her skin chill despite the heat.

"If you don't like the new subject, feel free to change it." He palmed her breast, molding the soft weight in his hand while his lips covered hers.

He might not be a good judge of character, but he had

a damn sharp eye for the heat between him and Jess. He knew she wanted him as much as he wanted her. He felt her comfort with him, her willingness to explore with him.

What an incredible gift.

He stroked her tongue with his, teasing a sigh from her. She pressed herself to him, her bare arms wrapping around his neck as she dragged herself still nearer.

She could have been pulling him into a riptide and Rocco would have gladly gone with her. Desire crowded his chest. He tunneled beneath her shirt to explore her naked skin, skimming his fingers along her ribs until he reached the swell of her breast. She cried out as he tugged down the cup of her bra and fingered the nipple. The texture felt so good he lowered his mouth to cover the tight point through her shirt. She tasted good even through the barrier of cotton.

Her hands hopscotched around his body, landing on his chest and then his waist. Then, without removing one stitch of his clothes, she cupped him through his fly, her fingers tracing the length of him again and again until he thought he'd explode. She peered at him through her lashes, studying his reaction as if he were her personal science experiment. Or as if he were back in her workshop, the guinea pig tester for whatever sensual torment she wished to try.

"Jess." His control teetered with this woman like no one else. He didn't want to restrain her hand, but for the love of Christ, she pushed his limits. "Stop."

Her hand paused, her panting breaths mingling with his in the dry air. A dog barked in the distance as they stared at each other, her heart racing beneath his hand.

"I want you on top of me."

Her request would be a simple one coming from any other woman. From Jessica, it came fully loaded with layers of significance. He willed himself to stay still. Steady. To give her time to change her mind even though that simple request moved him.

"Honey, I would love nothing more than to have you underneath me right now, but—" He didn't want to offend her. Wouldn't scare her for anything. But he had to be honest. "I'm so hot for you that I can't promise the sort of absolute control I'd want to have over myself for something like that."

"It will be okay." She was already rolling to her back. Already tugging on his shirt to bring him down on top of her. "Just try to look me in the eye sometimes."

Her hands were peeling off his shirt and moving down to his belt while he tried to process those words.

Look me in the eye.

He'd said he'd do anything for her pleasure, right? Surely he could accomplish something so simple. So basic.

So utterly intimate.

But any reservations he had were being teased away by the glide of her fingers down his shaft. She'd already unfastened her jeans and she lined up his cock with her belly, rolling him between her creamy skin and her hand.

Hunger for her rushed at him, barreling him over like a linebacker.

Yeah, he'd do anything this woman asked.

Pulling off her jeans, he ditched his khakis, tugging a condom from his wallet. He'd been through more prophylactics in a week than he'd used in...too long to contemplate.

Rocco stared down at her in the moonlight, her body

pale and delicate against the dark sleeping bag and the even darker roof.

"Are you sure?" He hovered over her, wanting this to be right for her. Remembering how he'd frightened her that first time at the Hotel del Coronado.

Their eyes met in the pale wash of light. Connected.

"I'm so ready." She wrapped her arm around his neck and arched up to him, dragging him down. "Come in and see for yourself."

He shuddered at the feel of her sex pressed to his. Hot. Slick.

The temptation to eat her up with his eyes was there, but he kept his gaze locked on hers as he touched her, spread her. Explored her sleek heat with one finger then two. And then he couldn't wait. Couldn't possibly hold off.

"Please, Rocco," she whispered, her lips full and lush and damp. "I want you to. Please."

Only then did he lower himself more fully against her, giving her more of his weight. Her softness molded to him, made way for him. And still he probed the depths of her dark eyes, watching for any hint of distress.

She gave none. Instead, she reached between them to wrap her hand around his cock and coax him closer. His eyes damn near rolled back in his head but he didn't shut them. Giving in to the inevitable, he tugged her hand aside and eased into her, fascinated by the way *her* eyes grew unfocused. The lids fell to half-mast and then closed completely as she tipped her head back, cried out his name.

He knew he'd never joined with a woman so fully. So deeply. A sense of elemental possession coursed through him as he seated himself inside her, holding himself there as long as he could before the need to withdraw and reenter grew too strong.

Her eyes widened again, her fingers clutching at his shoulders for one moment. When he thrust into her again—harder, faster—she made a small, mewling cry. But whenever she looked into his eyes he saw the same fire he felt, the same raw desire.

She wound her fingers through his hair and clawed lightly up his back. He nearly lost himself in the rhythm growing more fierce at her urging.

Part of him wanted to stand on the rooftop with her legs wrapped around his waist so he could feel the breeze all over his body as he claimed her, king-of-the-world style. But he knew that it was important to her to have him on top and he intended to satisfy her any way she wanted.

When the rhythm of her breathing changed, he paused to kiss her breasts and work the taut peaks one at time. She was so pretty, her body so supple and sweet.

He could feast on her all night if she'd let him. But right now, he wanted to give her that high peak, the shattering fulfillment of an orgasm she'd never forget.

"Jess." He changed his pace, speeding up again, taking her higher as her legs wrapped around his waist, holding him closer.

Sweat popped along his body and he didn't know how long he could wait for her. Her ankles jutted into his back and he couldn't think of a sexier place to feel a woman's foot. Every twitch and wriggle of her body tested his restraint. He wanted her with every breath in his being. Needed her.

Then her muscles started contracting, fluttering and

squeezing wildly all around him, and he was gone. The feel of her release triggered his, his whole life force seeming to flood out of him and into her. Waves of pleasure bombarded him until he shouted her name, his heart slamming wildly against his ribs.

He could hardly hear for his own ragged breathing, his pulse hammering his temples. But when some of that quieted just a little he became aware of another noise outside of him. A sound from somewhere out on the expanse of his property.

"What is it?" Jessica's fingers flexed against his chest and he wished he didn't have to worry her, but his every battle-honed instinct told him to be concerned.

Somewhere in the woods, Molly and Maggie were setting up a howl unlike anything he'd ever heard.

Reluctantly, he slid away from Jess, knowing her safety might depend on how quickly he acted.

"The dogs must have something cornered." He pulled on his pants, careful to stay low in case somebody was out there where he couldn't see them. "It could just be an animal, but it doesn't sound like it. There's a chance someone has breached the perimeter fence."

14

LIFTING HER spinning head from the kitchen floor, Leslie guessed Scott had an hour of freedom left at best.

After she'd regained consciousness from his right hook, Scott had forced her to reveal Jessica's whereabouts. Groggy and disoriented, she spilled her guess that Jess would hole up with the boyfriend on the neighboring ranch property. When she'd hesitated, the husband who'd vowed to love and honor her all his life had coerced the information by threatening to harm the runaway they'd taken in.

Not until that moment had Leslie seen how much he resembled her ham-fisted father. Scott Baylock was no better, controlling his wives with threats and pitting them against one another in a war for his affections. He just disguised his sexual abuse under the guise of marriage, and even that sham had been revealed when he'd had relations with the unwilling teen runaway.

But now, as Leslie listened to the commotion in the distance, she figured Scott Baylock would get his.

He'd gone after Jessica through the fence behind the duplex, assuming she had taken refuge there and angry at the thought of "his" woman with another man. The deranged son of a bitch. Leslie had let him go, knowing he wouldn't make it through Rocco Easton's security. She'd driven by the place and had seen the high-tech system arming the gate a few miles up the road. But Scott had been completely clueless, because he hadn't bothered to ask for her help.

How could he have turned his back on her so completely? Didn't he care about all she'd sacrificed over the years to help him get where he was? She'd thought he was different from her father, but over the years he'd morphed into the same exact man. Abusive. Controlling.

Now seemed like a fine time to let him hang himself with his own greed, and she couldn't deny taking a small amount of pleasure from the sound of snarling dogs a few hundred yards away. Better yet, the snarling dogs could be her ticket into the secured Easton property if she acted quickly. She'd already begun thinking about an *intelligent* plan to take Jessica. A plan Scott had never bothered to ask her about since he'd been so furious at the idea of selling his precious Jessica over the border.

What if Leslie followed through on the plan alone? Only, instead of bringing Jessica back to the Baylock family compound as a wife, she could truly dump her over the border? She didn't have to hurt her or sell her, although she'd gladly let Scott think as much to torment him. That is, if he survived those dogs. The desert would take care of Jessica for her.

Leslie had set herself up as Jessica Winslow easily enough. With the real Jessica out of the way, she could assume her identity for real. Permanently. She could pack up her sister wives and start all over again somewhere else with her new identity and pristine credit. They could get jobs and take turns caring for the other wives' kids.

They could have a chance at happiness without Scott.

Her head still pounding from the blow to her temple, Leslie went to the refrigerator to retrieve some steaks she'd purchased earlier. She'd thought out this part of the plan so carefully. Stumbling through the condo, she fished out a length of rope and some duct tape along with a handgun Scott had given her for protection.

In Scott's car she found two needles in his glove compartment that would be full of sedatives, drugs they'd used on that teen runaway, which might be helpful in making Jessica compliant. Stuffing it all into a leather backpack along with a pair of wire cutters, Leslie ran into the garage and hopped on the four-wheeler she'd purchased with one of the stolen credit card numbers before she'd passed them on to Scott.

It was the perfect vehicle for getting through the hole in the fence Scott had cut. Firing up the engine, she backed out into the dark and cut through the brush without the help of the headlight.

She felt more alive than ever. In control of her own destiny. With Scott cornered and a new identity calling to her, Leslie was only a few hours away from freedom.

Hitching the knapsack higher on her back, she just hoped Jessica cooperated.

"STAY HERE," Rocco ordered, punching his fists through the sleeves of his T-shirt as he straddled the four-wheeler inside his garage. "Call the cops and stay inside until they arrive."

She hooked her bra and nodded, nervous for him.

"Be careful." Leaning over the vehicle, she kissed him, then watched him speed away through the woods.

Spinning on her heel, Jessica ran from the garage and tore through the house to make the call. She didn't know where the light switches were, let alone his telephone, but she found her purse in the living room and pulled out her cell. She'd only just barely finished giving the police the information when she heard the four-wheeler come back again.

Hurrying outside, she didn't see Rocco at first, but she saw the shadow of the ATV by the garage. Maybe the dogs had just found an animal and he'd already taken care of it?

Listening carefully, she could still hear some canine whimpering in the distance. Turning to go back into the house, she was seized by two wiry arms. Woman's arms.

A blanket was slipped over her head like a hood, cinching around her neck and dragging her down. She cried out, but the noise was strangled and stilted for lack of oxygen. Clawing at empty air, she fell to her knees, the hood yanking her relentlessly to the ground.

Panic clouded her mind when she had to think. Her oxygen would run out. She needed to conserve air, but fear made her breathe deeper, her legs and arms spinning wildly.

A pinch jabbed her arm and she tried to pull it back, but now her captor—the wiry body—was sitting on her. Using body weight to hold her still. And the lack of air made it impossible to move—impossible to think.

The last image that raced through her mind was of Rocco and a fervent wish to have a second chance.

"IF YOU ARE who I think you are, those dogs are the least of your worries, asshole." Rocco left the shotgun on his four-wheeler and took the .38 when he saw the dogs had cornered a very human trespasser.

"You can't hurt me," the guy shot back, though he was careful to stay very still in deference to Molly, the more aggressive of the Akidas. "My kid hit a ball over your fence this afternoon and I was just trying to get it back."

"At midnight?" He wished he'd asked Jessica for a description of Scott Baylock. "You can tell it to the cops when they get here, but I can call the dogs off if you show me some believable ID."

The guy's sweaty forehead reflected the light from Rocco's four-wheeler, his skin pale and pasty with fear. He wasn't dressed for chasing balls into a neighbor's property in dark dress trousers and a white collared shirt. But then again, he wasn't dressed for purposeful trespassing either.

"I left my wallet back at the condo. It's just a few hundred yards back this way. You can call my wife and she'll bring it."

Rocco was second-guessing himself about the guy's identity until the man mentioned his wife. Something about the way he said it—a passing hint of ugliness in his expression—underscored Rocco's gut instinct.

He was talking to Jessica's rapist.

"What's your name?"

The pause was minor but significant.

"John Mandell." He reached to wipe the sweat off his brow and Molly leaped at his elbow.

"Heel!" Rocco shouted, bringing the dogs to his side instantly. Then, stepping closer to the other man, he motioned for him to hurry. "So take out your phone and call your wife. We'll put her on speaker and see if she thinks you're John Mandell too."

The guy didn't move.

"Or we can just wait for the cops." Rocco grinned, looking forward to unveiling this guy and his lying, impersonating wife too.

Beside him, Molly snarled and stilled, her attention fixed on a spot out in the woods to his right. With the four-wheeler idling behind him, he couldn't hear whatever she heard.

Could the wife be nearby?

"What is it, Mol?" Keeping the gun trained on his trespasser, Rocco leaned down to touch the dog's head and gave the command that would release her from his side, keeping Maggie with him to watch over the guy.

Molly darted through the brush at a dead run, but she was young and not as well trained, so for all Rocco knew she could be just going for a rabbit.

"I'll call home." Pasty-Face pointed toward his pants pocket. "If I can just get my phone."

Rocco nodded, listening for the police sirens that should be arriving soon. The local cops weren't close, but they should only take five more minutes, tops.

"Be my guest." Rocco waited, thinking about how much satisfaction Jessica would take from seeing this guy behind bars. The statute of limitations hadn't expired on the rape yet, but even if they couldn't convict him for that, he would be an accessory to the identity theft at the very least.

Actually, at very least, Rocco would beat the snot out of him.

The man started pressing buttons.

"You'd better put the thing on speakerphone now or I'll shoot it right out of your hand."

The guy fumbled and nearly dropped the phone, but he managed to hang onto it. Rocco stepped closer to hear whatever was happening on the other end of the call. Was he contacting Leslie? Or was there a chance he could have the wrong guy?

The cell rang once. Twice.

"Hello?" The feminine voice on the other end sounded terse. Pissed.

"Honey, it's me. John—"

"Scott, I don't know what the hell you think you're doing calling me after you—"

"Honey," the guy—*Scott*—cut her off. "This is *John*. I need you to bring me my ID out of the glove compartment in my van."

Rocco's heart pumped faster, fueling every cell of his body with fury. Disgust. This slime—this man at his absolute mercy in the middle of nowhere—was the same scum who had hurt Jessica. Not strong, grown-up Jess. But scared, vulnerable teenaged Jess.

His fingers flexed with the urge to wrap them around the other man's throat.

"Go to hell, Scott," the woman on the end fairly screamed. "I went ahead and took the sweet little dream girl you wanted while you were fucking up this plan from start to finish. If you want precious Jessica, good luck finding her in Tijuana."

The call disconnected, leaving an eerie silence in its wake. Rocco didn't understand what he'd just heard or how it could be true. But it was as if the ground had exploded under his feet for the second time in his life. He figured he looked just like pasty-faced Scott, with his mouth hanging open and his eyes wide.

Leslie Ann James Baylock—the bitch with the throaty voice who'd tried to seduce him—had Jessica.

"You'd better pray she's wrong, asshole." Rocco ripped the phone out of the guy's hands and jabbed the gun in his gut just as the sirens finally sounded in the distance.

Scott looked at him blankly, even when Rocco forced him to the ground. He'd leave him here for the cops to find because he wasn't slowing himself down carrying the raping bastard on his ATV.

"Leslie doesn't know what she's doing." Scott shook his head while Rocco bound his hands behind his back with a bungee cord. "She loves Jessica like a sister. I was going to make her a sister wife."

Rocco didn't know what the hell the guy was talking about and he wasn't sticking around to decode the ravings of some lunatic while Leslie had Jessica.

"Assume your wife is a hell of a lot smarter than you think." Rocco placed his boot on the guy's back for emphasis, not deriving any pleasure from seeing him squirm while Jessica was in danger. "Just tell me where Leslie might try crossing the border with a captive before I show you the first of seven ways I know to kill a man using just my pinky."

15

"YOU'VE LOST your mind." Jessica croaked out the words after being gagged for a good five hours.

She was basing her estimate of the time on the position of the sun in the sky—just pushing up the horizon at dawn. But her view was marred by her hair blowing in her face as she bumped along a dirt ridge on the wrong side of the Mexican border. She'd been tied to a four-wheeler for hours, racing through the sand and hills of Southern California and into Mexico.

Or she thought it was hours. Maybe it had been days. Everything had been fuzzy since she woke up.

"Girlfriend, I've just finally *found* my mind." Leslie slowed the vehicle to a stop in the middle of nowhere. Scrub brush and a few scraggly trees dotted a landscape made up of hills and ridges, red rock and sandy earth. There wasn't a house, a power line or a road anywhere in sight.

Jessica's whole body jerked forward as her impersonator cut the engine and hopped off. Leslie Ann tossed Jessica's duct tape gag on the ground and stared at her, roped like a calf to the ATV.

"Why are you doing this to me?" Jessica had to ask since the answer still mattered to her. Even through the layers of grime on Leslie's bare arms and the huge, ugly bruise on the side of her face, Jessica recognized the girl who'd held her hand after the worst ordeal of her life. An ordeal she'd been scared to confess to her own parents.

Only to find out her parents hadn't cared too terribly much.

Their reaction had made Jessica all the more resolved to stay in the foster system. She figured she'd be better off being close to her one friend—Leslie Ann.

"Scott loves you." Leslie Ann withdrew a knife from a knapsack on the back of her bike.

Jessica braced herself at the sight of the shiny steel, but Leslie simply bent over her bonds and cut through them, freeing her.

"Why did you marry him when you knew he did that to me? How could you?" Her body refused to make a grab for the knife or wrestle her captor for control of the ATV. Every muscle ached with weakness from the drug Leslie must have given her. From being tied in the same position for hours or days or who knew how long.

"I married him before you went out with him. Before you led him on until he couldn't stand it anymore. You and your damn sensual tricks." She wrenched the knapsack out of Jessica's reach as if suddenly remembering she'd left something important inside it. "Besides, Scott promised to take me away from my father."

"Why didn't you tell me he was your husband? How could you let me go out with him?" The questions sounded incredibly inane given everything else Leslie had done to her, but this woman had played a larger role in Jessica's rape than she ever would have guessed and she would damn well know why.

"He told me not to tell you. Or anyone. We planned to keep the whole thing under wraps until after I finished college."

"Until you dropped out." Leaving Jessica with no roommate, no explanation and no friend. "Did your husband hurt Rocco? Do you know where he is?"

She remembered the noise in the woods last night. Rocco going to see what had happened. Had it all been a distraction while Leslie Ann kidnapped her?

"Don't worry, hon. I think your boyfriend and his mongrels got the better of Scott." She pinched the bridge of her nose with her free hand and Jessica couldn't tell if she wanted to laugh or cry about it.

Maybe a little of both. Leslie Ann seemed to have been pushed beyond her breaking point.

But at least, thank you God, Rocco hadn't been lured into a trap. Maybe Scott would tell him where Leslie had taken her. Hope flared for a moment and then fizzled again.

How would he find her here, with no landmarks in a foreign country?

"I don't understand. Did you mean for Scott to be captured? If you would testify against him about the rape or how he's put you up to impersonating me—"

"I can't help you. Look, I'm sorry about what he did to you, but he was only trying to convert new wives into our mission." She withdrew something from her backpack and pointed it at Jessica.

A tiny, flipping handgun.

Nothing had prepared her for this. Not being impersonated. Not having this chick touch Rocco and steal from her. Not even being abducted. She was an idiot for seeing anything good in this woman.

"You're going to kill me because your husband is a lunatic?"

"Get off the bike." She gestured with the gun to where she wanted Jess to go. "And no, I'm not going to kill you. I'm giving you all of Mexico while I go back to the States and save my sister-wives from Scott. Maybe if he could have gotten over his obsession with you back then, things could have been different. But my chance at happiness with him is gone. All I have now are my sisters and I will do anything—anything—to protect them."

"Did Scott give you that bruise?" The swelling looked painful where the skin had cracked open.

Against all reason and very much against her will, Jessica felt a tiny pang of empathy.

"Yes." Leslie gestured impatiently with the gun again. "Get moving. I'm not going to let him hurt Carly or Tina or Rosa or any of the kids. And I'm going to help that poor runaway get back home."

Jessica stumbled away from the four-wheeler, her legs woozy under her while the gun followed her progress. The sand felt cool under her toes, reminding her she had no shoes to trek around the desert.

"Those are the other wives?" She gave up trying to understand the past and Leslie's decisions. Obviously, the woman had issues that had only grown deeper and more emotionally debilitating as the years passed.

Jessica would focus on what seemed most important to her and work from there. Maybe if she could convince Leslie she could help her, she could get a ride back to the States.

Back to Rocco.

Thinking of him made her heart constrict painfully.

"Three are his wives and one is a stray we picked up in the desert one night. She's just a teenage kid—no older than us when we met him." She straddled the four-wheeler and tossed a bottle of water to Jessica. "You have no idea what kind of hell I've saved you from as a Baylock wife. I didn't see it until tonight, but somewhere along the way Scott turned into my father."

Switching the gun from her right hand to her left, Leslie Ann kept the weapon trained on Jessica as she started the vehicle.

"You can't leave me here!" Jessica forced her legs to close in on Leslie, ignoring the gun.

"Stop!" Leslie fired at the ground, sending up a spray of sand at Jess's feet. "I don't want to hurt you, but I will if I have to. I need time to start over somewhere else, and I need your identity to do it until I can come up with something better."

Spitting dirt out of her mouth, Jessica felt panic close in on her as she realized the implications of being left out there with only one bottle of water.

"You can't do this. Rocco will make sure no one else uses my identity. You've been reported to the cops. You left fingerprints all over my apartment."

Leslie tossed Jessica a thin blanket that might have been the hood she'd nearly suffocated her with earlier.

"The years have made me a whole lot smarter than you remember, but thanks for the tip." And with a rev of the engine, her former friend and psycho impersonator took off, spraying a rooster tail of sand and gravel in her wake.

She was on the wrong side of the border with no passport, no ID and no sense of direction save the sun.

Gathering up the blanket and the one bottle of water, Jessica began to follow the ATV tracks, hoping like hell Leslie knew how to get back into the U.S.

No way would she wait for Rocco to bail her out of this one. She'd walk until she had to chase the buzzards away, but she wouldn't allow any Baylock to get the better of her this time.

"I TOLD YOU that you should be a cop, Roc. Your lead brought the police to a whole polygamist enclave."

Rocco's buddy Lazarmos had been on the phone with him half the night, helping him coordinate his efforts to find Jessica. Rocco turned up the speaker on his cell and left it resting in his shirt pocket while he cantered through the hills toward the Mexican border. He'd debated taking the ATV or the Appaloosa, but the horse was better over unfamiliar terrain and could always find his way home if Rocco needed to call for a helicopter for Jess.

The thought of her hurt closed his throat. She'd dealt with enough at Baylock's hands without having to fight his wife for her identity.

Her life.

"So the cops found a whole slew of wives in the location Baylock gave us?" He kept talking because it helped keep his mind off all the things that might have happened when Leslie Ann stole Jessica right out from under him. There'd been signs of foul play—the discarded needle and some scuff marks on the sidewalk—but there'd been no blood.

A fact that kept him hoping.

"Actually, they found three confirmed wives, four alleged kids and one scared-as-hell runaway from Arizona whose parents have been searching for her for weeks." Lazarmos had put Rocco in touch with his uncle the cop, and the police had followed up on Baylock's info about the whereabouts of his illegal family.

As a polygamist, the guy had kept his clan in hiding under different names over the years, but he'd squealed pretty quickly to the local cops when they'd found him peeing his pants trying to keep away from Molly and Maggie.

"I hope they can nail the guy on charges if he touched a minor." Anger rumbled through him at the memory of what he'd done to Jess. If the police couldn't prosecute Baylock on the old rape charges, maybe he would still do serious time for hurting the runaway.

"You've gotta head a few degrees east, man," Laz instructed.

Back in San Diego, Laz had a locater fix on Rocco's cell phone using a gadget he'd delivered to the Dulzura house at about three o'clock that morning. Now, Laz was following Rocco's progress toward the border with the tracking device, guiding him toward the last known location of Leslie Ann's cell. The wireless provider had agreed to help out when the police leaned on them.

Apparently, Leslie had checked in with her extended family—the women Scott had called sister-wives—shortly before dawn.

Now, long after noon, Rocco rode south and turned a few degrees east, wishing they could have gotten more help from the Border Patrol. The border guys were keeping an eye out for both women coming back into the States, but their numbers were thin and their coverage was strapped even on a good day.

"Laz, I'm going to shut off the phone to save the battery." Rocco wanted to speed up anyhow. "I'll check in again in about twenty minutes."

"Roger that. Good luck, man."

Rocco switched off the phone, telling himself he had to be on the right path because he couldn't think anything less. Jess had believed in Leslie Ann—or at least believed the woman had some decency in her—long after Rocco had said she was up to no good.

He'd thought maybe it was naiveté on her part, but after seeing the way Leslie Ann had been coerced into doing her husband's bidding, he wondered if Jess might have understood her better than he'd realized. Maybe she'd be able to talk Leslie Ann into giving herself up.

Or at least could convince her not to use deadly force.

The possibility made his heart stutter and anxious thoughts crowded his brain, the antithesis of the clear-eyed focus he'd employed as a SEAL. Was it because he'd been out of the service for a while?

No.

He knew the gut-tearing fear he was experiencing now had everything to do with his feelings for Jess. Feelings he'd wanted to ignore since he didn't want to care about anyone too deeply when his head wasn't even screwed on straight.

Too bad his response to Jess had been raw and primal— too instinctual to be stopped by something so misleading as logic and good intentions.

Miles passed. Scrub brush scratched his arms. Rocco urged on his horse, a swift and sure mount who could navigate her way without much help from him.

His eyes scanned the deserted hills and occasional gas

station or roadside souvenir stand for any trace of Jess. He'd give anything to find her alive and unharmed. He'd make any sacrifice to hold her again—whole and healthy and full of life.

He'd accept any terms she wanted to give him if she would have him in her life, including closing doors on the repo business. It didn't matter half as much as being with her.

Then again, he'd stay away from Jess forever if that was what she wanted. He'd make the biggest sacrifice of all if only he could find her before anything happened to her.

16

JESSICA WANTED to stop and sleep, her feet so heavy she swore she couldn't pick them up even one more time.

The drug she'd been given stuck with her, making every move sluggish. She could die out here and it wouldn't even take very long. Stubbornness alone kept her going. That and the determination to see Rocco again. To prove to him she could save herself.

Or maybe she just needed to prove that to herself.

Hot sand had blistered her soles long ago. By now, the blisters were cut and bleeding right through the pieces of blanket she'd torn off and tied around them. She wore the rest of the blanket on her head like an Arab sheikh. Even though she was sweating like a pig from the heat, she couldn't afford to fry her skin when she could be out here for days.

Her thoughts of an Arab must have given rise to her first hallucination. She spotted a mirage in the distance, a horse and rider galloping through the shimmering heat. The white and russet horse bore a tall, broad man with a turban or whatever it was called. The ends of it flapped against his shoulders.

And, oh God. She knew those shoulders.

Was he real?

Relief nearly brought her to her knees and still Jessica feared he would disappear when she got closer. She ran toward him, the makeshift bandages falling off her raw feet.

The horse thundered toward her, the rumble of hoofbeats on the ground assuring her this vision was real.

"Rocco." His name was a dry croak from her throat.

He vaulted off the horse's back, landing a few feet in front of her. He wore his T-shirt tied around his head, the back covering his neck and the tops of his shoulders. He was no mirage. Just the most amazing repo man come to repossess her.

She smiled at the thought as she almost fell into his arms. Her footsteps felt strange and then her knees went wobbly.

And oh shit. She wanted to prove she didn't need saving and yet she seemed to be fainting at his feet.

"She's gonna be fine, Ricardo. You'll see."

Rocco's father patted a bench in the waiting room of the Scripps Hospital the next day. The ambulance had taken Jessica here and they'd kept her overnight for observation, shutting Rocco out of the room since he wasn't family.

He hated hospitals. The antiseptic smell of the waiting area made him nervous, bringing to mind other medical centers. The VA hospital where they'd flown him to have his foot put back together. The Catholic facility where his mother had died.

It had to suck for his father, too, but he appreciated the old man's quiet presence, even now that he knew Jessica would be okay. His father had arrived at the hospital within half an hour of Rocco's call, the quick response reassuring Rocco that his father's faculties definitely weren't slipping away altogether. He'd force his dad into seeing a specialist to make sure they could preserve his mental clarity for as long as possible.

But right now, Rocco's thoughts were for Jessica.

Her pulse had been thready when she collapsed against him, her skin washed out and cold despite the heat. Apparently the sedative Leslie Ann administered had been a dose for someone twice Jess's size—a common problem with illegally obtained drugs.

While the SDPD had been hunting down Leslie Ann James Baylock, Jessica had reclaimed her identity through sheer grit. Still, he was thankful the cops had arrested Leslie Ann trying to sneak into the Baylock compound to see her sister-wives.

Rocco planned to do everything in his power to make sure no one ever hurt Jess again. Even if she didn't want to be with him anymore, she'd have his protection for the rest of her life. He had to put all those SEAL skills to some kind of freaking use now that he was out of the service.

"Rocco?" A nurse appeared in the waiting room carrying a chart in one hand and rolling some kind of hanging IV with the other.

Rocco turned and his father stood, tossing aside the magazine he hadn't really been reading.

"That's me." Rocco strode closer to the door, sidestepping an empty wheelchair. "Can I see her yet?"

"We're discharging her, actually. Are you the responsible party?"

"My boy is very responsible," his old man chimed in,

clapping Rocco on the shoulder. "A retired Navy man, you know. He'll take good care of her."

Yeah, he definitely needed to start taking better care of his father too. Anthony Easton deserved the best treatment options Rocco could find.

"Where is she?" Rocco wanted to see her *now*. To find out for himself if she was well enough to go home.

He hadn't slept at all the night before, remembering what her feet had looked like. Remembering the bone-chilling fear when she collapsed that she'd died.

He wouldn't take an easy breath until he saw her.

"Her room's right down here." The nurse turned along one of the hospital's endless white corridors.

"You go take care of her, son." His father backed away, letting Rocco see Jessica alone. "You'd better bring her for dinner soon though, you hear? I want to meet this one."

The last words had to be shouted since Rocco was six rooms down the hall by then. The nurse turned again and then pointed to her left.

"Right here. She's already signed the paperwork if you'll just wait for an orderly."

And there she sat.

In the middle of a hospital bed, Jessica waited for him fully dressed, her feet dangling a few inches above the floor. She wore her pink T-shirt with the angel on it, although her jeans had been traded for pants that looked like hospital scrubs. The cuffs had been rolled up to allow for bandages and some sort of makeshift shoes fitted over the cushiony gauze around her toes and heels.

"Hi." She grinned at him, making him realize he'd been staring at her, speechless.

"You look incredible."

She laughed, a sound he wanted to get down on his knees and thank God for. Holy hell but she'd scared him.

"I don't know about that. The hospital shampoo was only one small step above dish soap, but I'm just happy to be clean."

"I'm thankful as hell you're alive." He'd been so worried about her, but she looked perfect. Healthy and happy and so alive his chest hurt with gratitude.

He wanted to sit down on the bed with her, to scoop her up in his lap and hold her against him. Feel her heart beat next to his. But he didn't know if he should or how she felt about this. Him.

He'd marched right in to claim her today as if he was family, even though she'd never given any indication she'd be sticking around after her impersonator was caught.

"Thank you for saving me." Her words caught him off guard. They sounded far too polite. Formal.

And he had to put an end to that right now. This was the woman he'd made love to on a rooftop. The woman who looked as at home in his stables as she did teaching belly dancing.

"I didn't do jack shit to save you, lady." He sat down on the hospital bed beside her, shoving aside a tray with a water pitcher and some flowers that looked to be from her office assistant. "Do you know how far you walked with oozing feet and drugs pumping through your veins?"

She shook her head. "I could hardly put one foot in front of the other."

"Twelve miles."

"It seemed like a thousand."

"Jess, you were like a kick-ass action figure. Do you know you were almost to the border?"

Outside the room, a wheelchair rattled down the hall and rolled to a stop outside the door. Rocco waited for the orderly to wheel it in, but no one appeared.

He went to the door and looked down the hallway in time to see the back of his old man's head disappear down a corridor.

He grinned and wheeled the chair into the room, more than ready to break Jessica out of the hospital.

"Looks like your ride's here."

She nodded.

"Thank you. I appreciate you coming to get me. After this, I promise I'll be out of your hair—"

His heart stopped.

"Don't." Rocco let go of the chair and sank back down to the bed, covering her lips with his finger. "Don't even think about kicking me out of your life again."

"Mmpf."

He released her lips.

"I wasn't going to. I just wanted you to know that after you give me a lift home, I don't plan on needing any more rescues. If you want to see me again—and I hope you do—it won't require any SEAL skills."

His heart kicked in again, the relief so strong his legs damn near gave out.

"How about cop skills?" He inched the chair close to the bed and reached for her, eager to have her all to himself.

She put her hand on his chest, not letting him pick her up.

"What do you mean cop skills?"

Rocco scooped her off the bed and plunked her gently

in the chair before settling her flowers on her lap. He studied her for a moment, thinking he would see her like this again one day when he wheeled her home after their first child.

"I mean I've been doing some thinking about going into police work." He wheeled her out of the room, waiting for her reaction.

When Jessica didn't say anything, he spelled out the plan.

"You know I've been tossing the idea around. My friend Laz has an uncle on the force—"

"You don't need to know anyone. Any police department would be lucky to have you." She twisted in the chair to look at him as he took her down in the elevator.

Could he blame anyone but himself if she liked the cop idea?

"I know, but it's good to have friends in a new career and I think I'd be good at it. Plus I'd be a respectable guy again. No more stealing cars in the middle of the night." God, he'd miss it.

He nodded to a guy who held the front doors for them and then wheeled the chair down a sidewalk until he was parallel with his truck.

"Hold your flowers." Bending over, Rocco lifted her out of the seat and carried her through the parking lot.

Being a cop would be an easy trade-off if it won him Jessica.

"Rocco?" She waited while he tucked her into the passenger seat of his truck and settled her flowers at her feet. "Do you think you need to be a cop for my sake?"

And with that loaded question, he shut the passenger door and jogged around to the driver's side. He wanted to tread carefully because if she told him to take her home right now—to *her* home—he'd lose his freaking mind. He didn't think he'd recover from yesterday until he could hold her in his arms all night for at least one night. Then hopefully for a whole lot more.

Settling himself in the driver's seat, he slid the key into the ignition. Jessica's hand covered his and held it.

"Are you?" she pressed.

"Wouldn't you like it if I went back to a less…furtive profession? I know how you feel about repo men."

She slid closer to him on the bench seat.

"I learned something about myself yesterday when I was walking those twelve miles that seemed like a thousand." Her fingers smoothed across the back of his knuckles, her smallest touch turning him on. "I learned that image doesn't count for much when you're fighting for your life and that—no matter how many luxury retreats I lead or how tricked out I make the Escalade, at the end of the day, I can't change the core of who I am. And you know what? Neither can you."

"But I'm more than a repo man, Jess." He didn't get what she was driving at. "Just like you're more than a foster kid."

"I know. But if we like those parts of ourselves, I don't think we ought to feel compelled to hide them under anything else."

The message became clear. And really, incredibly sweet.

"You don't think I should be a cop?"

"I think that a man who christens his tow truck has found his calling in life. Maybe all that sneaking around stuff you did as a SEAL is still in your blood."

Seeing himself through her eyes touched him. His voice dried up so damn much he didn't trust himself to speak for a minute.

"What do you think?" she prodded finally, her hand reaching up to stroke his jaw. "I also had an idea for giving some less expensive workshops geared toward single and working mothers. I think right there's a big market who need to get in touch with their sensuality, and maybe they'd appreciate a more stripped down, cost-effective approach. No taffeta. No candelabras."

"You're so freaking priceless." Rocco wrapped his arms around her, crushing her to him. "Please come home with me, Jess, and let me show you how incredible I think you are."

Jessica nuzzled his chest, burrowing close.

"Okay, but I don't think my feet are ready to revisit the roof."

"First-floor sex only," he promised, already picturing her spread out on his bed, her wild red hair spilling in every direction.

"Mmm. I like that idea." She nipped at his neck and then licked the spot. "Did I mention I got a new idea for a workshop while I was in bed this morning? Maybe you can help me try it out. It involves ice cubes and cinnamon flavored mints…."

* * * * *

THOROUGHBRED LEGACY
*The stakes are high when it comes to love,
horse racing, family secrets
and broken promises.*

*A new exciting Harlequin
continuity series coming soon!*
Led by New York Times *bestselling author
Elizabeth Bevarly*
FLIRTING WITH TROUBLE

Here's a preview!

THE DOOR CLOSED behind them, throwing them into darkness and leaving them utterly alone. And the next thing Daniel knew, he heard himself saying, "Marnie, I'm sorry about the way things turned out in Del Mar."

She said nothing at first, only strode across the room and stared out the window beside him. Although he couldn't see her well in the darkness—he still hadn't switched on a light...but then, neither had she—he imagined her expression was a little preoccupied, a little anxious, a little confused.

Finally, very softly, she said, "Are you?"

He nodded, then, worried she wouldn't be able to see the gesture, added, "Yeah. I am. I should have said good-bye to you."

"Yes, you should have."

Actually, he thought, there were a lot of things he should have done in Del Mar. He'd had *a lot* riding on the Pacific Classic, and even more on his entry, Little Joe, but after meeting Marnie, the Pacific Classic had been the last thing on Daniel's mind. His loss at Del Mar had pretty much ended his career before it had even begun, and he'd had to start all over again, rebuilding from nothing.

He simply had not then and did not now have room in

his life for a woman as potent as Marnie Roberts. He was a horseman first and foremost. From the time he was a schoolboy, he'd known what he wanted to do with his life—be the best possible trainer he could be.

He had to make sure Marnie understood—and he understood, too—why things had ended the way they had eight years ago. He just wished he could find the words to do that. Hell, he wished he could find the *thoughts* to do that.

"You made me forget things, Marnie, things that I really needed to remember. And that scared the hell out of me. Little Joe should have won the Classic. He was by far the best horse entered in that race. But I didn't give him the attention he needed and deserved that week, because all I could think about was you. Hell, when I woke up that morning all I wanted to do was lie there and look at you, and then wake you up and make love to you again. If I hadn't left when I did—the way I did—I might still be lying there in that bed with you, thinking about nothing else."

"And would that be so terrible?" she asked.

"Of course not," he told her. "But that wasn't why I was in Del Mar," he repeated. "I was in Del Mar to win a race. That was my job. And my work was the most important thing to me."

She said nothing for a moment, only studied his face in the darkness as if looking for the answer to a very important question. Finally she asked, "And what's the most important thing to you now, Daniel?"

Wasn't the answer to that obvious? "My work," he answered automatically.

She nodded slowly. "Of course," she said softly. "That is, after all, what you do best."

Her comment, too, puzzled him. She made it sound as if being good at what he did was a bad thing.

She bit her lip thoughtfully, her eyes fixed on his, glimmering in the scant moonlight that was filtering through the window. And damned if Daniel didn't find himself wanting to pull her into his arms and kiss her. But as much as it might have felt as if no time had passed since Del Mar, there were eight years between now and then. And eight years was a long time in the best of circumstances. For Daniel and Marnie, it was virtually a lifetime.

So Daniel turned and started for the door, then halted. He couldn't just walk away and leave things as they were, unsettled. He'd done that eight years ago and regretted it.

"It *was* good to see you again, Marnie," he said softly. And since he was being honest, he added, "I hope we see each other again."

She didn't say anything in response, only stood silhouetted against the window with her arms wrapped around her in a way that made him wonder whether she was doing it because she was cold, or if she just needed something—someone—to hold on to. In either case, Daniel understood. There was an emptiness clinging to him that he suspected would be there for a long time.

* * * * *

THOROUGHBRED LEGACY
coming soon wherever books are sold!

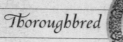

Thoroughbred *Legacy*

Launching in June 2008

A dramatic new 12-book continuity that embodies the American Dream.

Meet the Prestons, owners of Quest Stables, a successful horse-racing and breeding empire. But the lives, loves and reputations of this hardworking family are put at risk when a breeding scandal unfolds.

Flirting with Trouble

by *New York Times* bestselling author

ELIZABETH BEVARLY

Eight years ago, publicist Marnie Roberts spent seven days of bliss with Australian horse trainer Daniel Whittleson. But just as quickly, he disappeared. Now Marnie is heading to Australia to finally confront the man she's never been able to forget.

The stakes are high when it comes to love, horse racing, family secrets and broken promises.

A new exciting Harlequin continuity series coming soon!

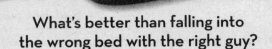

REQUEST YOUR FREE BOOKS!

2 FREE NOVELS PLUS 2 FREE GIFTS!

HARLEQUIN®

Blaze™

Red-hot reads!

YES! Please send me 2 FREE Harlequin® Blaze™ novels and my 2 FREE gifts (gifts are worth about $10). After receiving them, if I don't wish to receive any more books, I can return the shipping statement marked "cancel". If I don't cancel, I will receive 6 brand-new novels every month and be billed just $4.24 per book in the U.S. or $4.71 per book in Canada, plus 25¢ shipping and handling per book and applicable taxes, if any*. That's a savings of 15% or more off the cover price! I understand that accepting the 2 free books and gifts places me under no obligation to buy anything. I can always return a shipment and cancel at any time. Even if I never buy another book, the two free books and gifts are mine to keep forever.

151 HDN ERVA 351 HDN ERUX

Name	(PLEASE PRINT)	
Address		Apt. #
City	State/Prov.	Zip/Postal Code

Signature (if under 18, a parent or guardian must sign)

Mail to the **Harlequin Reader Service:**
IN U.S.A.: P.O. Box 1867, Buffalo, NY 14240-1867
IN CANADA: P.O. Box 609, Fort Erie, Ontario L2A 5X3

Not valid to current subscribers of Harlequin Blaze books.

Want to try two free books from another line?
Call 1-800-873-8635 or visit www.morefreebooks.com.

* Terms and prices subject to change without notice. N.Y. residents add applicable sales tax. Canadian residents will be charged applicable provincial taxes and GST. This offer is limited to one order per household. All orders subject to approval. Credit or debit balances in a customer's account(s) may be offset by any other outstanding balance owed by or to the customer. Please allow 4 to 6 weeks for delivery. Offer available while quantities last.

Your Privacy: Harlequin Books is committed to protecting your privacy. Our Privacy Policy is available online at www.eHarlequin.com or upon request from the Reader Service. From time to time we make our lists of customers available to reputable third parties who may have a product or service of interest to you. If you would prefer we not share your name and address, please check here. ☐

HB08

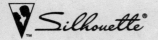

Romantic
SUSPENSE

**Sparked by Danger,
Fueled by Passion.**

Seduction Summer:
Seduction in the sand…and a killer on the beach.

*Silhouette Romantic Suspense invites you to the hottest
summer yet with three connected stories from some
of our steamiest storytellers! Get ready for…*

Killer Temptation
by **Nina Bruhns;**
a millionaire this tempting is worth a little danger.

Killer Passion
by **Sheri WhiteFeather;**
an FBI profiler's forbidden passion incites a
killer's rage,

and

Killer Affair
by **Cindy Dees;**
this affair with a mystery man is to die for.

Look for

KILLER TEMPTATION by Nina Bruhns in June 2008
KILLER PASSION by Sheri WhiteFeather in July 2008
and
KILLER AFFAIR by Cindy Dees in August 2008.

Available wherever you buy books!

Visit Silhouette Books at www.eHarlequin.com   SRS27586

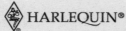

HARLEQUIN®

Blaze™

COMING NEXT MONTH

www.eHarlequin.com

HBCNM0508